PRAISE FOR JANE CIABATTARI'S
*STEALING THE FIRE:*

*"Stealing the Fire* reminds me of Grace Paley's *Enormous Changes at the Last Minite.* There is the same fascination with the turning points in 'ordinary' lives, and with the h·· ·sions which accompany them. Like Paley, Jane C·· f the spare, no-nonsense narrative voi·· le, invites you to drop everything ä The tug between feeling and reasor. ..he edge."
—Carol Brightman, autho. ..y: Mary McCarthy and Her World

"In these stories, characters often mark a rare event in the world around them—two full moons in July, the worst drought of the century—if only to note a momentous occurrence within their own lives, and in Jane Ciabattari's hands, each of these stories becomes itself a rare and wondrous event."
—Greg Sarris, author of *Grand Avenue* and *Watermelon Nights*

"These are graceful, honest stories about people coming to terms with loss. Jane Ciabattari writes with sensitivity and heart."
—Molly Giles, author of *Rough Translations, Creek Walk and Other Stories* and *Iron Shoes*

"Jane Ciabattari's absorbing, reality-based stories recall the best fiction of Joan Didion and Robert Stone. Whether the location is Silicon Valley or Central America, they are contemporary, tough-minded tales for these difficult times."
—Grace Lichtenstein, author of *Machisma: Women and Daring*

STEALING THE FIRE

# STEALING THE FIRE

*Stories*

Jane Ciabattari

**CANIO'S EDITIONS**
Sagaponack, New York

"Stealing the Fire" first appeared in *The East Hampton Star*; "The Almost-Perfect Man," "Gridlock" and "Totems" first appeared in *Redbook*; "A Pilgrimage" first appeared in *Denver Quarterly*; "Once in a Blue Moon" first appeared in *Blueline*; "Memorial Day" and "Wintering at Montauk" first appeared in *Hampton Shorts*.

The author wishes to acknowledge the generous support of the New York Foundation for the Arts, The MacDowell Colony, the Virginia Center for the Creative Arts and The Writers Room; and the editorial counsel of Canio Pavone, Nohra Barros, Sally Arteseros, David Milofsky, Sheridan Sansegundo, Anne Mollegen Smith and Barbara Stone. Thanks also to Molly Giles, Susan Harper, Betty Hodson, Lorre Sintetos and Jane Vandenburgh, who share a love of the craft of fiction, and to Ann Banks, Gwenda Blair, Carol Brightman, Caroline Casey, Lesly Curtis, Jeanine Johnson Flaherty, Kathryn Kilgore, Ellen Levine, Grace Lichtenstein, Denise Low, Mary Marchetti, Terry Pristin, Robin Reisig, Anthony Russell, Harvey Shapiro, Marilyn Webb and Galen Williams.

Published in the United States by
Canio's Editions,
P.O. Box 552, Sagaponack, NY 11962.
(631) 537-1825.
canioseditions@peconic.net


ISBN:1-886435-11-1
Library of Congress Cataloging-in Publication Date is available upon request.
Printed in the U.S.A
10 9 8 7 6 5 4 3 2 1
First Edition

for Mark

If there is a limit to all things and a measure
And a last time and nothing more and forgetfulness,
Who will tell us to whom in this house
We without knowing it have said farewell?

—Jorge Luis Borges

# CONTENTS

# STEALING THE FIRE

DORA'S FATHER DIED in San Francisco, on a Monday night in late August when the setting sun lined up opposite the moon rising full over the Bay. Driving home from the hospital after he was gone she was nearly blinded by the unaccustomed direct light at rush hour. There were a number of collisions that evening; people drove into concrete dividers and smashed into cars in oncoming lanes. It seemed the universe had gone awry.

His death had been no accident. Two years before, when Dora was eighteen and had gone to live with him, he already knew his heart was failing.

"Don't ever let them bullshit you," he'd said after one meeting with his doctors. "Listen to your gut." But she couldn't.

She hadn't really expected him to die.

Her father was as intent on his death as on a novel he was creating, watching it happen and working at it with all his skill. His material was the incremental failing of his own flesh, his immense sorrow at knowing that every moment passing was ushering him toward the end, his rage at the doctors and the fear he felt, his pain at leaving her behind.

In April he was so short of breath he couldn't walk more than a few steps without stopping. In May he began turning blue around the edges—she noticed it first in his fingertips and lips. He couldn't go far without his oxygen supply.

In July he worsened. Her mother and the doctor pressed him to try surgery. The four of them sat in his living room with its view of the ocean shuttered against the light. Her mother gave all the reasons he should do it, and he responded with all the arguments he had against it. Then the doctor listed all the things that could happen next if he didn't have the operation.

"You don't have to end up an invalid," the doctor concluded. "After the surgery you could resume a full teaching load, maybe even play tennis again."

"Okay," he said at last, gasping for air, the crease of pain growing between his dark brows. "Okay, okay."

Her mother and the doctor sat back, satisfied. He looked at Dora, his blue eyes flat with defeat. Dora felt her own heart beating, steady and strong as a fist pounding against the cave of her chest. Surely he could hear it. If she'd had a heart to spare, she would have given him hers. Why wasn't it a kidney he needed? Bone marrow. Blood.

She pushed her hand hard against the spot over her heart to muffle the beating. Touching it made her feel like crying. She forced herself to hold the tears back. Her mother fell to pieces when he talked about dying.

"I don't want Bette around," he said. "She gets me so upset I have to comfort her. Destroys my concentration."

After her mother and the doctor left she told him about the spot that hurt.

"In oriental medicine it's the place of grief," he said. "You'll feel that again after I'm gone." For years he had dabbled in Eastern thought—Tibetan

Buddhism, Zen. "You won't need me," he added. "A terrible wind may come. Demons and wild animals may pursue you. Face your fear. Pray for compassion and the clear light will come. Then one day you'll walk in pines and find the leavings of birth. You'll be fine."

"How can you be so sure?" She couldn't imagine him not being there.

"Something I learned a long time ago," he said.

"Right." She rolled her eyes. She hated it when he talked about the sixties as if it were all about love and mystical revelation. She knew better.

Her mother always said she left him because he was a burned-out hippie wino deadbeat. He would disappear into the desert for weeks, chewing peyote with some shaman. Or he'd drive over to Reno, rent a motel room, order Bushmill's from room service and beat away at his typewriter until he ran out of money. Then he'd come roaring home and her mother would nurse him through the crash. She had to set up secret bank accounts all over town. Things got worse after Dora was born in 1967, the year he published his first novel. The reviewers dubbed him "the psychedelic Rimbaud." That, her mother said, was his license to stay stoned for the rest of their marriage.

After that celebrated first novel had come a second. The critics called it incoherent. The third he never finished.

Dora didn't remember much about those early years. Once when she was five her parents gave a party and her father waltzed her around until she was dizzy, singing "Devil in the blue dress, blue dress, blue dress." The music was loud, the haze of incense and candles and smoke was thick, the house grew dark as the night wore on. "Wig hat baby," he sang, holding Dora high in the air.

Suddenly a tall man with a rust-red beard jostled him from behind. "Hey you!" he shouted. "Better not mess with my old lady again." Her father put her down and turned to face the redbeard. "Not here," he said, low and angry. They ended up on the front porch slugging it out. "Cool it, cool it," her mother kept yelling. No one noticed Dora standing there in the darkness.

Her mother asked him to move out after that. Her love for him ebbed as surely as he lost oxygen in the end. When Dora was seven, her mother married a contracter named Vern who had moved to Squaw Valley to work on the Winter Olympics and stayed on. Dora didn't pay much attention to her mother's stories about her father's drinking until she hit fourteen and woke up every morning ready to explode with tension, and discovered firsthand the cozy appeal of alcohol. Her mother began to say, "You're just like him," and it wasn't a compliment. She figured sooner or later her mother would throw her out, too.

After a near-fatal accident driving across the border into Nevada at the wheel of a crowded car, her mother sat her down for a long serious talk about ruining her future. Her stepfather suggested she try earning her own keep. He said it would give her a sense of responsibility. She got an after-school job at a cafe in Truckee. She tried to be good, but every time she'd get to feeling overwhelmed by things, which was often, she'd go get wasted.

"But why?" her mother would ask, catching the telltale signs she'd been drinking.

She would shrug. "It's the only thing that makes me happy."

Despite the number of days she was absent or spaced out after a hard night, she finally made it through high school. After graduation her mother sent her to San Francisco to live with her father. "You got it from him, let him straighten you out," she said.

Her father was clean by then, saved by his failing heart. He ate carefully, played tennis every other day and took a wide range of prescribed medications. He set a strict no-more-drinking rule.

"You mean if I follow your shining example you'll kick me out?"

"I had to give it up myself."

"Why? If you didn't when she wanted you to?" If her mother had just waited a few years, they'd all still be together. He could quit for himself, but not for them.

"It's too late for me to be a father," he said. "But I can teach you everything I know."

He enrolled her in his writing workshop and appointed himself her secret tutor. He gave her extra writing assignments. He talked about discipline and courage and opening up to the dark side. He made writing seem as solitary and illuminating as meditation.

When she read her stories aloud to him, he seemed puzzled that her work bore no resemblance to his. He seemed to expect a familiar echo, or at least a variation on his themes.

"Why do you begin at the end?" he asked one day. "It kills the suspense."

"What happens isn't the point," she said.

"What then?"

"Language. Memory. How one phrase, one thought triggers another, which triggers another."

"Is that why you tell your stories in bits and pieces?"

"That's how I think."

"Maybe that will change," he said. He didn't say stop. He said her work was raw, but that she seemed to be finding her voice. Originality of voice was what gave good writing its power, he said. He prescribed William Blake, Walt Whitman, Kerouac, Bellow's *Augie March*. They were okay, but she couldn't imagine herself writing *On the Road*.

"What about the women?" she asked.

"Try Virginia Woolf." Dora liked her. Especially *The Waves*, and her diaries.

"Writers of genius create sentences as distinct as fingerprints," her father said one day in his workshop. There were eight of them around the seminar table. Dora always sat across from him so she could watch his face closely. No one else knew he was ill. When the pain was bad he would wince and say he'd just come from the dentist.

"Hear Faulkner's rhythms," he said that day. He read for a few minutes from *As I Lay Dying* in his resonant voice. Every time he frowned she wondered if he was hurting. She chewed her lower lip in sympathy.

At the end, he gave the class the exercise of typing a passage from *Absalom, Absalom* that began: "He would just have to write 'I am your father. Burn this' and I would do it." It was one of his riddles, and this time it really bugged Dora.

"What's the point?" she shot at him later. "Fathers don't have that kind of power these days."

"Don't be so sure. Just do it and see what happens."

She typed it over and over in a fury until she could see the words on the page at the end of that day as she tried to drift to sleep without a drink to slow her anxious thoughts. What happened was she was pissed off—Who was he to tell her what to do?—and even more determined to figure out how to write stories her own way.

"You don't have to worry about being original," he announced one morning late in the semester as they sat drinking coffee at the kitchen table.

"Is that a decision or a decree?" she teased. At home she wanted him to be a father, not a teacher.

"I've been thinking about it," he went on. "You have a voice. You were born with it. That's why you chose me." As if he deserved credit for teaching her, or being her father. It was hard to say what he meant, and she didn't want to ruin the implication of progress by asking.

After she turned in her next story, he said, "Keep going, even if you hate it. Something will come of it, sooner or later." Was the story that bad? Was this another game?

In her stories people disappeared, attachments dissolved, nothing lasted for long. The most important things were never said out loud.

Dora was proud that her father talked to her about dying. She learned to hide her fear of it. As he weakened, she tried to be strong.

"I don't want them to touch my heart," he said.

He believed the powerful vulnerable organ that gave rhythm to each moment and connected him to life was sacred. She believed it, too.

During the summer he showed her drafts of stories he was writing. In each of these he had a child—a baby son, a daughter ten years old, a teenage son, a daughter in college. In the stories he loved his children more than he could tell them.

In late summer, as his energy faded, he turned to poetry. In one poem he was the keeper of the Word who defied the gods by passing his knowledge on to his girlchild. He broke the taboo, risked death for her, and after he was gone she was left to wander in shadows. Disturbed, she brought the manuscript to his bedside. "What do you mean?"

"I'm having crazy dreams," he said. "It must be the new medication. Last night I dreamed I was being held captive in a cage lined with mirrors. When I'm gone you'll have to steal the fire for yourself."

His words came with such difficulty she could barely hear him. He settled back into sleep, a frown of frustration on his face. More and more he talked in riddles. She couldn't tell if it was the medicine or the exhaustion or some awful wisdom that came with dying.

---

Just after dawn on the day of his surgery, her mother called to say she couldn't make it to the hospital. The house Vern had built for them, which was at the entrance to the Valley, had burned to the ground in the night. Dora could feel the dry, blasting power of that fire as she stood at the telephone in her father's kitchen in San Francisco, staring at the fuzzy grey line that separated the layer of fog above the Pacific from the brightening horizon. No, she thought, no. She couldn't do this alone. She wanted to stop the day.

She saw him a few hours later, under sheets on a gurney in the hallway.

"I have a writing assignment for you," he said hoarsely. "Write a story about things. Find the meaning in the meaningless." Another riddle.

"Things?"

"You know, objects. Things. By this time next week I want you to have a new story to show me."

She nodded, not understanding, eager to please.

Then he said, "I'm only forty-seven." She held his hand, kissed his dry cheek, tried to find words to acknowledge the look of fury in his eyes.

"I'll see you later," she said fiercely, willing him to survive. "By the time you get home I'll have that story."

"I opened him up and his heart was so fragile it gave way beneath my hands," the surgeon told her. "Just gave way when I touched it." He seemed to want Dora to absolve him, but she had no words. The spot above her heart was beginning to ache.

That's why her father had put off the surgery for years. He knew. This was the terrible ending he'd been dreading all along.

He'd written a long letter to her mother with instructions about what to do with his things. He'd left it on his desk in a sealed envelope addressed to Dora. She opened it and read it to her mother over the phone.

He left Dora his house and everything in it, and enough money to finish her last two years of college. He asked to be cremated and buried in Squaw Valley. He wanted the memorial service to include readings of a Wallace Stevens poem that ended, "things go round and again go round," and a passage from *The Tibetan Book of the Dead*.

He'd been preparing all this and the writing assignment for Dora on the night of the fire.

The house Vern had built in the Valley after he married Dora's mother had been as carefully constructed as a puzzle box, design within design. It was octagonal, with a deck, a garden, a low Japanese-style bridge over a brook. Dora had lived there happily for years, from the time she was eight until the wildness came upon her and the fights with her mother and Vern began, and the push to be like her father took over.

She thought of that beautiful house in ashes and wondered if her stepfather in constructing it had left some chink in the chimney, some fatal flaw to keep her mother with him on her father's last day, leaving her to handle things on her own.

When Dora entered the valley at ten-thirty the morning after her father died it was hot and still. She had left the fogged-in coast before dawn, driving inland through hundreds of miles of dry farmland, then climbing into the foothills of the Sierra Nevada, through Emigrant Gap and Donner Pass to the narrow canyon where her father's ashes would be buried.

Toward the end of the drive, at the higher altitudes, she could feel her blood singing in her veins like the vibrations of train tracks signaling an arrival far in advance. Then granite peaks closed her off from the rest of the world.

She stopped at the edge of the Valley to see the house. As she stood in the ruins of the sunken living room where the couch had once faced the fireplace, she heard the flapping of wings. These were not feathered wings. Something heavier. A bat. She went closer to the charred fireplace and saw in the shadows just inside the chimney a gathering of ash clinging to the surface. The inverted creature there was incinerated in the posture of sleep, wings wrapped around it like a shroud, feet gripping still, the silvery death's head barely holding its form. If she touched it, even exhaled softly, it would fall apart.

That evening she ate dinner with her mother and Vern at a place along the river. Her mother had dark smudges beneath her eyes, and the skin at her temples was transparent as rice paper. Her stepfather looked solid and healthy in his red flannel shirt and expensive cowboy boots. He was her mother's buffer; Dora had no one.

She picked at salad and grilled trout and drank mineral water, trying not to look at their glasses of wine. Her mother kept up a nervous monologue about rebuilding the house.

"Yesterday Vern said we should do it on the same spot, but today he looked into it and discovered that if we sold the land and took the insurance money and built on a higher lot the resale value would be increased. I don't know if I really want to rebuild where everything we love went up in flames . . . ."

She shrugged, and looked at Vern, who had been putting away a steak and baked potato and glass after glass of red wine, interrupting her only to throw in a figure—"We'd come out fifty or sixty grand ahead," or "I could get it for less then twenty percent down."

The tension of not talking about her father left Dora with a throbbing headache. When Vern went off to pay the check, she asked, "Is everything set for the funeral?" Her mother's eyes filled with tears.

"The funeral director here is very kind," she said. "We'll set up a buffet in his back parlor after the service. We don't have any place for it because of the fire. People from the university keep calling. A group of them are coming." She stopped. "How are you holding up?"

"None of this feels real. I can't think, I can't sleep."

"I wish you'd come stay with us." She seemed sincere, but Dora didn't trust her.

"I'll be better off alone."

Dora held herself carefully so she wouldn't cry as they walked out of the restaurant. She said no to their offer of a lift to the place they had rented for her. She wasn't sure about Vern's driving. He had the heavy-eyed look of a man about to drift into unconsciousness. She headed the few blocks up the mountainside on foot, glad for the cold and the moon to light her way.

The rented cabin was part of a cluster built for skiers. It was comfortable, with maple furnishings and rust-colored carpet, a Franklin stove to take the edge off the cold. Her mother had stocked the kitchen with bread, cheese, fruit, milk, coffee, juice, mineral water. Not a beer or bottle of wine in sight. She was doing her part.

Dora lay sleepless through the night—short of breath, altitude alert—thinking about the final words she'd heard her father say, the anesthetic sleep, the plunge of the surgeon's knife, his heart exposed to air. And now was the time for the final burning. She couldn't bear to think of his body in flames.

It was daylight before she was able to fall asleep at last. Sirens woke her at noon. Another fire. The Valley was tinder dry after thirty months without rain, and covered with a fine layer of pine pollen—nature's extra seeding to balance the trees lost to the drought.

"Write what cannot be said," her father had said when she was haunted by nightmares in the weeks before his operation. She could still hear his voice, deep and measured. The answer was to work on his assignment. But she couldn't.

Instead, in the late afternoon she hiked high up on Squaw Peak, hoping to quiet her mind with steady exertion—climbing from boulder to boulder, focusing on the placement of her feet and hands, the pendulum of her weight, her breathing, the sharp smell of pine. Jeffery pine smelled like butterscotch; the cones of the Ponderosa were armed. Her father had taught her that.

Toward the top she found the discarded eggshell of a spring-hatched bird, tiny as the last joint of her little finger. Somehow this fragile thing, original shelter of a bird long since flown, had stayed intact on the side of the trail for nearly half a year. Her father had been alive when the feathered creature pushed its way soft-boned and wet from this shell, but he had been losing ground already then, beginning the dying. Seeing the eggshell, she could feel the ache just above her heart. She could hear his voice. "Find meaning in the meaningless." This thing in her palm, this remnant of birth, was dry and dusty, soon to be ground back into the earth, and the once half-formed creature inside it now soared above the Valley, seeking by instinct the lift of the strong thermal currents.

Looking down, she found the spot along the tree-line above the road where the fire had been. The house Vern built was now a smudge on the landscape. It had been a massive and complicated thing; it was gone now, leaving only memories, imaginings. What if she had stayed in this Valley and pushed her wild streak into the oncoming lane? What if she had never had the chance to know her father? What if she had ended up with his curse but not his gift? The questions rattled away as she picked her way down the trail.

It was night. Her father was out of reach. She couldn't even remember his voice. She got in the car and drove to the house. In the spot where her room had been was a tangle of charred beer cans and pint bottles. She had hidden empties in a secret place behind the wall in her room, where her mother couldn't find them. Somewhere in that mess was an amber bottle she had kept to remind her of her first taste of beer, on a camping trip with her father the summer she turned fourteen. The sweet musty taste of warm Tecate had taken away her shyness, and they had really talked for the first time. She told him she wanted to be a writer, too. The empties had piled up beside the tent over that weekend. He taught her to scratch the labels off the bottles with her fingernails, and bend the empty cans in half.

Her unfortunate mother had ended up saddled with drinkers on all sides. But she knew how to cut her losses. She'd written Dora off as surely as she had her father. It just took longer.

Dora went back to the car, bought a cold sixpack at the 7-11 and drove along the narrow mountain roads for hours with the radio on a country station, opening the fliptop cans one-handed. Up switchbacks and down, headlights cut, she burrowed into the darkness, singing along with the lonesome songs.

As the sun followed its path the next morning Dora dreamed she was writing her name on her father's skin.

He was coaching her. Here, he would say, pointing out a good stretch of skin just beneath his collarbone. Try it here. Then, with good humor, how about down my arm?

She woke around noon with a cottony mouth and a nosebleed. It was the altitude, the infernal dryness. Her sensitive skin giving way to the force of her own pulse. It was her first hangover in nearly two years.

At the funeral that afternoon as the minister spoke the last words over her father's ashes (he said, he said, he said, but she could not hear), she sat rigidly and stared out the glass wall of the chapel at the whirlwind of dust behind the pulpit, expecting the voice of thunder to split the air, signaling the end. When the service was over, tiny droplets fogged the glass. Rain at last.

But she could not weep. Even at the gravesite as they placed his urn in its dark square of earth, her body held her grief inside. Afterward, standing beside a small table overflowing with food and wine, she listened as the others in his department spoke of his having a gift that never came to full flower.

"How's your mother holding up?" one of them asked. She couldn't respond to the polite phrases; the hot tongue of fury was in her throat. She was being treated like a child. The funeral service had followed her father's plan, but he had made no place in it for her. She was the one who stood by him. She knew him better than anyone.

When it was finally over, she brushed away Vern's invitation to dinner and retreated. She lay flat on the wooden deck of the cabin, pounded her fists and wept. Where was he? She still needed him to guide her. But there was no one. She had to begin by herself, do it the only way she knew how. She brewed a pot of coffee and sat down at the wooden table to work.

The next day she went back to the edge of the Valley as night fell, returning to that burned-out place that had once been her home. She started a fire in the fireplace with the day's newspaper, kindling, chunks of fallen beams.

First to go was that incinerated clinging blind creature in the chimney. She released its terrible grip with one swipe. She thought of her father's face, gray and unblinking in his final days, focused inward. He'd never really seen her. And she couldn't know him until she'd fought the pull of language and booze in her own blood and won.

Once the wood caught, she added the story she had written all that long day and night, a story about things she had found in the Valley, and the meanings she had given them, and the memories she had dredged up. It was fifteen pages filled with words, told in fragments, going sideways. Her final message to her father. You were my teacher. This is the last story I'll write for you. You were my father. I am who I am.

The top page caught first, charring at the edge, giving up to the flame. Then the rest was on fire. The manuscript was an organic thing opening outward, creating a blackened frame—living layers of ash around the tiny flickering center, its burning heart.

Once the fire burned past its peak, subsided, cooled, she brushed the ashes into a pile and carried them with her as she drove out of the Valley through the newly wet fields to the sea, where she scattered the dark memory of the story on the beach where she had walked with her father many times, before she could tell a story of her own.

# TOTEMS

BETH SAT STIFFLY in the cramped bus seat, staring out the window into the darkness. Her eyes kept jumping to the freeway signs and the lights of distant towns, straining for a familiar detail. But the stretch of highway beyond Seattle was empty and the blackness closed in around her.

She felt exhausted, disoriented. Things were happening too fast. The Canadian airport employees had gone on a wildcat strike. Now it was eleven in the evening. She and Phil should have been in their hotel room by now. Instead they faced a miserable three-hour bus ride to Vancouver, God knows how much longer to their hotel.

They had learned just before takeoff that planes would not be allowed to fly into Vancouver because of a strike. Normally this bit of news wouldn't have bothered her; she'd have found an opportunity for adventure in the change of plans, at least have seen the extra traveling time as a chance for a deep satisfying talk with Phil, free from the daily details that took up so much time. They had spent countless excited hours in cars, planes, trains, making plans and sifting through the past together, but this time the anticipation of strange places frightened her. She was still recuperating from the miscarriage she'd had six weeks before. Still weak and weepy and easily rattled. Any diversion from the expected left her with a throbbing headache, unlocked fearful thoughts. She had been trying hard to remain calm these past weeks. Why had she let Phil talk her into this trip? She felt safer at home.

Suddenly the bus entered a tunnel. Beth gripped the seat in front of her. When they came out the other end she saw strange structures with red blinking lights across the field. This is ridiculous, she told herself. Just relax and let it pass. There's nothing to be afraid of.

All she could make out of the other passengers were the tops of heads, coughs, fragments of conversations breaking around her. Phil dozed at her side, giving in easily to circumstance. She wished she could sleep, too, but something forced her to stay alert. When she closed her eyes the motion and odor of the bus dizzied her and the pain in her head expanded so it filled the void. At least with her eyes open she could divert herself. She wished it were daylight; then she could see the countryside they were passing through.

She bent over, struggling with nausea from the diesel fumes, and pulled her purse onto her lap. Balancing it carefully, she searched for the rock she had brought along. Just as they were leaving home for the airport she had decided she wanted to take something small and intimate along on the journey. At first her eye had been drawn to the mauve-and-yellow Russian Easter egg she kept on her desk. But it was too fragile. Instead she had chosen a serpentine rock she had picked up one day at Baker Beach. It was round and jade-green and worn smooth. Serpentine changed form depending upon its water content. In seawater and fog it was soft, fluid; in dry air, unyielding. Now, as she held it tightly against her palm in the darkness, it warmed to her hand.

She turned to watch Phil's profile. Her head throbbed. Poor Phil. He'd thought a trip would take her mind off her grief. As if it were that easy.

After she got out of the hospital, Beth tried to tell him how it had hurt; she tried to explain the process as she experienced its echoes. The cramping pains, then the laboring to produce heavy clots. The emptiness when it was over. The sadness at not having a child that was his.

And why? A minute hormonal fluctuation? A fleeting disloyal thought lodging in her womb, emptying it? After waiting so long for the "right time," when her daughter Rebecca was old enough to handle it, when her new marriage was secure enough, had she betrayed herself? Was it possible she was not as eager to have Phil's child as she had thought? Was it possible she could not, would never have his child? She was a detective, entangled in ifs and maybes. If only she hadn't stayed out so late the night before. If only she'd stopped working the moment she'd realized she was pregnant. If only she hadn't blown up that night when Phil hadn't like the fish she'd made. She'd had a flash-point temper in those early weeks of pregnancy. If only she'd been able to stay calm, a serene vessel.

Maybe she should have insisted on having this baby when she was younger. Maybe thirty-seven was too late. Maybe she shouldn't have given in to Phil's plans, his idea of an organized life. Maybe, just maybe—and this she would not allow herself to say to him—maybe it was Phil's fault. How could she think such a thing? Maybe he thought it was her fault. "Do you think it was my fault?" she asked him over and over in different guises. She knew she was being tedious, but she couldn't stop herself.

"Don't dwell on it," he said. "We'll try again. Think of the future." But she couldn't. She felt empty and ashamed. Phil had been a good father to Alex's daughter for ten years now. She'd seen a new look on his face when she'd told him about his own child to come. Now it was gone.

"It's over," her doctor told her. "Forget about it." As if that were possible.

Finally, exasperated, helpless, Phil ran out of comforting words. "We won't talk about it anymore," he said. She accepted this rule, seeing the logic in it, but she couldn't stop her mind from racing. The burden of secret worry grew within her.

One morning he found her in the bathroom squeezing coils of toothpaste onto the floor. "That's how I feel," she said, trying desperately to make him understand why she couldn't forget so easily. "Squeezed out."

"My God," he said, grim with shock and horror. "Get hold of yourself."

For a moment she could see herself through his eyes and she was horrified too. After that she tried to keep her mind blank. On Saturdays, while Rebecca was playing baseball in the park and Phil was teaching, she'd escape to the beach and lie in the sun, concentrating on the ocean rhythms as she felt the muscular tightening within that had gone on for weeks after the first pains. Sometimes at night, when she was half asleep, the pain would confuse her and she would think it was happening all over again. Remembering, she would weep quietly, huddled away from Phil.

At the beach she withdrew from the sunning mothers. She sat on a sandy hill above them and watched the sailboats, the green hills of Marin County across the way, the shadows of gulls flitting across the sand. Here there were no demands. No conversations to attend to, no decisions to make.

Staring at the Pacific, the salt breeze in her face, she envisioned tidal waves, the earth below her opening in a spasm to engulf her, undertows sweeping her downward, hair trailing. This beach was unsafe for swimmers; it had a sharp drop-off, rip tides, vicious cross currents, occasional sharks. The Golden Gate Bridge was just around the corner to the right, beyond granite walls that the children scaled like monkeys. Her eyes followed the comings and goings of dogs, fishermen, lovers, children. She felt detached from them, as if she were watching a movie from the balcony.

When they reached Vancouver at two in the morning, the bus terminal was deserted. Blinking, they were herded through bright, empty corridors. Beth clutched Phil's arm. She wished for nothing so much as a warm bed.

As they went through customs she'd feared a weapon would materialize in her purse and she'd be detained. Phil pushed her ahead in the line when she hesitated. "And you're with him?" the official asked. She nodded. That was all. He waved them through. They looked safe enough.

Outside, Phil sprinted ahead and opened the door of the last vacant taxi. Inside, she leaned back against the seat and shut her eyes. They were almost there. She brightened with relief. The headache and tension faded. The city sparkled with colored lights reflected on empty, rain-slick streets. She hoped it was as beautiful in the daylight.

The hotel was vine-covered and square; it reminded her of a college dorm. She followed Phil in a fog through a dim hall to a pool of light around the reception desk. As he registered she glanced down another hall, which was lined with heraldic crests. Above two stained-glass doors at the end was a sign: "Tilting Room." The words seemed incongruous. A tilting room. Was that like the fun-house where she had seen Phil grow smaller and smaller, until he seemed to barely come to her knees? Was it an arena for the sort of jousting tournament she'd seen in a Robin Hood movie? She asked the clerk.

"The tilting room? It's the bar." She laughed. It made sense, in a roundabout way.


She was swimming, treading water far out to sea. She had shepherded all her loved ones into a supertanker for safekeeping, and alone she awaited the catastrophe. A rocket had misfired and was expected to crash into the ocean. When she sighted it, she went numb with fear; it was huge, half as large as the earth's circumference. It approached ever so slowly. Then it hit the water, and the waves from its impact exploded the supertanker. Those she'd expected to be safe were catapulted into the sea.

Heavy currents carried her along with the rest. Some could not swim. She was able to grab and hold onto a child. Then she realized that Phil couldn't swim well, and that if she held onto the child, she could not expect to save him. As she watched, the shoreline gave way before the force of the water. Struggling to hold the child in a circular embrace, she let the waves batter her and carry her along.

A voice filled the air. "You must toll the bell."

"But I don't know where it is," she replied.

"There, behind you."

"I can't," she cried out.

"You must," boomed the voice. "You are the *carillonneur*."

"No!" She woke with a cry, struggling against the dream. She heard a weird, strangely melodious whistling noise. She tried to relax and let it roll over her in waves, to use logic on the night fears. It was the sea wind. Imaginary danger. A nightmare, not real. She thought she heard heavy breathing, cautious footsteps. Someone coming for her? She felt weighted down with fear. Trembling, she turned to hold on to Phil.

"It's okay," he whispered groggily, still far away from her. His heartbeat steadied her until she could sleep again.

In the morning, Beth awoke before Phil did and tiptoed to the window for her first glimpse of English Bay. She saw people in tweed coats strolling along the sea wall looking pink cheeked and healthy.

Later she and Phil breakfasted on scones and marmalade and tea and set off in the weak spring sunlight for a walk through Stanley Park. It was a weekday, and the park belonged to mothers with baby carriages, retirees, the tennis crew. The paths were lined with hyacinths, tulips, jonquils, flowering cherry trees and rhododendrons. Swans nested on the banks of Lost Lagoon, sitting on huge thatches of straw on little islands near the shore. Peeking into one nest, she saw four huge eggs dotted with fluff from the mother.

Toward noon they reached the totems. The sun beat on her face, hot now, and soothing fingers of wind lifted her hair. There were eight totems, mammoth and eloquent. Craning her neck, she studied the figures. Eyes. Wings and eyes. Grimacing snouts and bared teeth.

She read the legend: "The totem was the British Columbia Indian's 'coat of arms.' Totem poles are unique to the northwest coast of British Columbia and lower Alaska. They were carved from western red cedar and each carving tells of a real or mythical event. They were not idols, nor were they worshipped. Each carving on each pole has a meaning. The eagle represents the kingdom of the air; the whale, the lordship of the sea; the wolf, the genius of the land, and the frog, the transitional link between land and sea."

Phil had wandered off into the woods nearby. It was silent except for the sound of a bird, whose whistle was like the wind, wailing, or a keening for the dead. Water glistened on both sides of the promontory. The mountains beyond were topped with snow. Squinting, Beth blanked out the pieces of civilization—the piers, buildings and factories—and saw only totems, trees.

She had expected to feel frightened by the totems. Instead she felt comforted. They were ageless and potent. They towered above, reducing her to human scale. She had only the power of one. In another time she might have had the healing presence of a group, of ritual.

One of the totems drew her. The sign said it was a mortuary pole; the top was hollowed out to contain a coffin. She liked the fierceness of the carved faces, the green around the eyes, the sharp pelican beaks, the ghostly sweep of the eagle's wings. The other poles were more polished. This one was weathered. Its fangs were bared. The bottom animal, the green-eyed frog, held a manlike infant between its legs.

The transitional link. Frog-child, unborn, incomplete, floating in amniotic fluid, choosing its moment to let go, oozing out with its bloody accompaniment. And there was no explanation. The frog-mother's face grimaced in pain.

This totem satisfied Beth's perception of terrible gods. She was no longer afraid. What had happened had been worse than anyone had allowed it to be. Ifs and maybes were useless. There would never be an explanation.

Tension eased from her neck and shoulders, and she realized she'd been holding herself as if expecting a blow. She stood quite still, waiting for what came after. She felt she was on the brink of knowing what she had to know to go on. The sound of the shrill, wailing bird stopped.

She reached into her purse for the hard green serpentine rock, and placed it gently at the foot of the totem. Then she turned and walked back to look for Phil.

# A PILGRIMAGE

THE FIRST DAY Catherine was back in Mexico City she went to the cathedral on the Zocalo to pray. The bells were ringing, calling the faithful to noontime mass, as she stood in the strong mountain sunlight, a slight, fine-featured woman with pale skin and auburn hair shot through with gray. Her simple linen dress was the color of ashes, and the deep blue shawl she wore around her shoulders echoed the color of her eyes.

Looking up, she could see the man who was orchestrating the sound, the throbbing bass tones and lighter, harmonizing treble. The bell ringer was only a fraction of the size of the statue of Justice on the roof, and this struck her as appropriate, the human tiny in comparison to the ideal.

Inside, a priest was saying mass at the gilded Altar of Forgiveness. Catherine covered her hair with her shawl and stood in the back, adjusting to the darkness. Then she moved on, past Our Lady of the Sorrows, Our Lord of the Cocoa Bean, the Altar of the Kings. There were dozens of possibilities here for the pious.

She passed a chapel with a black-skinned Jesus over the altar. Banks of red and white carnations, and a red velvet banner covered with offerings—paper money and small golden hearts—drew her eye. The small chapel was crowded. Curious, she stood in the arched doorway. An old woman with a face that seemed to have been dusted lightly with flour handed her a leaflet with a prayer to be offered to *"La Milagrosa Imagen de*

*Nuestro Señor del Veneno*." Our Lord of the Venom? The poison? Surely that was wrong. Her Spanish was good, but this was a word she had not encountered before. It was frustrating not to know its meaning, yet it gave her a perverse pleasure: one more mystery to ponder in this country she loved but did not always understand. She tucked the prayer into her purse and moved on down the dim stone pathway.

And there, in simple contrast to the others, was the chapel of Our Lady of Guadalupe. Catherine had seen Guadalupe's image before, in grimy bus stations and humble roadside grottoes as well as in the great cathedrals of Mexico and Central America; she had seen her modeled in plaster and tin as well as in gold filagree. She knew that to her people Guadalupe was not a distant ethereal figure; she was a living force, dwelling among them, touched daily by their suffering. She was mother and refuge to even the most unfortunate. Today Catherine was drawn to her as if to an old friend. She knelt, feeling at home. Guadalupe would make a fitting companion in the days ahead. *Buenas tardes*, Catherine whispered. I am traveling alone for the first time in a strange land, and I have a long journey ahead of me. Watch over me, please. Bless my mission of mercy.

Guadalupe's kind face seemed to lighten in a smile. Catherine smiled back. Do you hear me? Am I worthy of your attention? Perhaps they were choosing each other. Catherine lingered, resting her head in her arms, then made her way back to the Zocalo.

Walking along the Calle Guatemala she passed an old-fashioned barber shop with mirrors and tiled walls and a ceiling fan with wooden blades.She had gone to a barber shop like this with Gregory in the late forties, when he had been sent here to launch a branch of his bank. He sat in a high red leather chair beneath a poster of an Aztec warrior with a feathered headress, poised on one knee with a bow and arrow ready to shoot. Catherine, watching from another red leather chair, held her breath as the barber stood with the straight-edged razor poised over her fair-haired young husband's delicate throat. "I kept thinking, what if he slipped just a fraction of an inch," she told him that night at dinner.

"You're being silly, Cat," he said, squeezing her hand.

Another time, as she walked down these narrow streets past the university, a pack of school boys dogged her trail, smacking their lips and making obscene noises. "It's their way of showing appreciation for your beauty," Gregory told her.

"Why can't they leave me alone? I've done nothing to encourage them."

"You're a woman and American. That makes you a target. Ignore them."

She shivered now in the sunlight. These past months she had felt so alone without Gregory. She had spent the whole of her adult life with him. She was an only child, a late-in-life daughter of a wealthy couple, raised in San Francisco and schooled there at the Convent of the Sacred Heart. The world had opened smoothly for her, a narrow sunny pathway. Gregory was ten years older, an officer stationed at the Presidio, when they met. She was drawn to his air of assurance and his wit. She allowed him to carry her away from the shelter of the church into his own, more worldly sphere. They had lived in Buenos Aires after Mexico City, and finally had settled in Atherton, an hour south of San Francisco, when he was brought back to the home office as a senior vice president. He had planned to retire early, and take her back to Mexico for an extended stay. Then his heart gave out with no warning, just before his sixtieth birthday.

One moment she and Gregory were sitting on the patio as they did each morning, drinking coffee and reading the newspaper, the only interruption the calls of the birds and the sound of tennis balls from the courts nearby. The air smelled sweetly of mock orange. The next moment Gregory was lying on the tiled floor, his face rigid with pain, and the sunny days were over.

Catherine took the metro to the Bellas Artes stop, and found her way to a hotel she remembered for its court-yard restaurant. She was flustered as she ordered *enchiladas verdes* and coffee, but the waiter was patient with her. Humor, gentle eyes, a knack for disarming had always been her allies in this country.

Gregory spoke precise Spanish with a Castilian accent and an intensity that seemed to disturb many Mexican men. Catherine had never studied the language, yet she could make herself understood nearly as well as he after their years in Latin America. She came to it on her own, in her dealings with the people. She would speak in English first, using the normal tones of the transaction at hand, and then in her imperfect Spanish. The first words she learned were "*gracias*," "*con permiso*," the graceful phrases to use with strangers to smooth the way.

The sky was deep blue above, the tablecloths pink over yellow, the floors and fountain tiled in blue and yellow. Flowers in a dozen shades of pink were banked in the corners of the courtyard. She felt drenched in color. The waiter hovered nearby to fill her coffee cup as soon as she emptied it. She sat peacefully in the sunshine and thought of all the days she sat like this on the patio at home. Birdsong and lazy mornings. She spent decades in a comfortable cocoon. Her life could never again be like that. She had to get used to being alone. From now on, she made her own path. She was proud of the steps she was taking to make a place for herself in the world. This trip. Her mission.

The man at the next table reminded her of an old friend of Gregory's. Raul had been a Mexican diplomat. The last time she had seen him was in 1954, when he and Gregory had an appointment at the Maria Cristina Hotel. She came along to drink coffee and watch the peacocks wander in the lush gardens. A high-ranking Mexican official joined the men. At diplomatic gatherings, Catherine had always found him courtly and attentive, so she was surprised when he greeted her curtly and directed her to a table some distance away. She toyed with the lumps of sugar and stirred her coffee in its lapis-and gold-edged cup and gazed at the strutting birds. Gregory sat stiffly, smiling with his mouth closed, the way he did when he was agreeing to something because he knew he had no choice. Later he had told her, "We go home next week." When she questioned him, all he would say was that the government had changed. It was not as hospitable as it once had been toward American business. The bank was no longer welcome, and neither were they.

The waiter brought her the check. Across the courtyard a man in a dark suit was reading a newspaper with the headline, FIDEL CASTRO HERIDO. Castro shot? Killed? She was not sure.

After Gregory died, she came awake each morning at two or three, her heart beating wildly. She was filled with inexplicable guilt. She wanted to think of Gregory safe in some afterworld. She wanted to think she could join him some day. She wanted to believe, but that once fertile area within her was barren now. When she reached for familiar prayers, she remembered only isolated phrases. Seeking solace, she began attending mass at a little church in Menlo Park. Father Pietro, the priest there, was willing to hear her concerns. Inside her was a despair so strong that her own will was powerless against it. She thought of herself as a delicate plant turning toward the sun, pores open; it could warm her, or burn her with blazing intensity. Desperate for comfort, she was intent on being receptive to an image, a gesture, a sign of some sort that might restore to her the possibility of faith.

And then, unexpectedly, like a fever breaking, Rosa came into her life. When Father Pietro learned

Catherine spoke some Spanish, he asked her to volunteer at the church's refugee center. The people there needed food, shelter, money, papers—things Catherine took for granted. Then he sent Rosa to live with her. From the moment she saw her, a frightened and withdrawn twelve-year-old with a graceful body and haunted eyes, she and Rosa were bound together.

Rosa's brother disappeared one night. His body was found at the bottom of a ravine near their village. Her mother had not allowed Rosa to see, but she overheard whispered details of the mutilation. The following week, her mother paid a man to smuggle Rosa out of the country with five others from her village. Her mother did not know she had made it to safety.

Rosa could not sleep more than a few hours at night. When she woke, screaming for her mother, Catherine brought her warm milk and held her in her arms. After spending time with the troubled girl, Catherine would lie awake herself, her thoughts of Gregory mixed with images of slaughter she could not absorb. Over the weeks, the helplessness she felt became unendurable.

She began to pay attention to news accounts of the troubles in El Salvador. Attacks by death squads were so routine that the newspapers used brief items giving the number murdered as fillers. The politics of the country had changed since she and Gregory had visited San Salvador years before on bank business. The situation seemed confusing, but there was no doubt in Catherine's mind that a government that would initiate murder, or fail to prosecute it, was evil.

A journalist who had traveled in the countryside and seen refugee camps set up by the church came to speak at her parish. Afterward, Catherine questioned the visitor. Had she been near Rosa's village? When was she going back? Could she look for Rosa's mother?

"Sorry, but I'm not going back," the woman said. She was small and compact, with short ash blonde hair permed into a halo and a deep tan. She was dressed simply in a black pantsuit. There were olive-brown circles under her dark eyes. "Journalists are targets now," she said. "I had a couple of close calls myself."

"What do you mean?" Catherine pressed.

"Rounded up in the night, blindfolded, driven around, threatened, that sort of thing."

She seemed so young—barely into her thirties— and yet she spoke casually of the danger of reporting what she had seen. Catherine had a glimpse of another sort of path. It took courage.

Catherine began to drive into San Francisco to visit a refugee center in the Mission District, trying to find people from Rosa's village and inquire about her mother. The third week she showed up, the director asked her to translate the stories the refugees told and type them up to add to the documents being gathered to help them gain asylum.

Catherine entered a land of horror. She spoke with an eleven-year-old boy with electrical burns all over his body, a fifty-year-old grandmother who had been raped repeatedly and her teeth knocked out because her husband taught at the university. The stories she translated reflected a brutality beyond her understanding.

One night she dreamt she was in an airport waiting for people to get off a flight from San Salvador so she could board the plane herself. Through the metal doorway came a man on crutches with an improvised bandage around his head, and another man with a missing arm and black smudges where his eyes had been. Then came a woman with a gaping hole in her face carrying a child with missing hands and an agonized expression, and after them a string of young men with their heads split open. Catherine sat, her heart pounding, horrified. People around her were talking, drinking coffee, reading the newspapers. She nudged the woman next to her.

"Look at that," she said. "What is happening down there?"

The woman looked at her blankly.

"Don't you see them?" Catherine pointed at the bloody procession. The woman shook her head warily and moved away.

When Catherine awoke, she felt she had been given a sign. Someone has to do something, she thought. I can make a difference. I know people down there.

That morning she said to Rosa, "What if I were to go look for your mother?"

Rosa stiffened in fear and shook her head. "You'd be killed."

"You don't need to worry. I'm an American. They wouldn't dare bother me. Maybe I could even bring your mother back with me, or arrange to have her come. Would you like that?"

"That would cost lots of money."

"I have enough."

"It is a dangerous place."

"I know."

"I'm not sure where she is," Rosa sobbed. "I don't even know if she is alive."

"She must be. I will find her."

Catherine began to plan a trip southward. Keith begged her not to go. "If Dad were alive, he wouldn't hear of it. Have you lost your mind?"

"This is exactly what he would do. Go to San Salvador. Speak with the top people. Get some action. Haven't you heard him say that a thousand times?"

Keith laughed despite his frustration. "You're right about that. But aren't you doing enough at the refugee center? I worry about the way you are allowing yourself to be drawn into this mess. Before you know it, you'll find yourself on all sorts of lists for subversive activity."

"There's nothing suspect about what I'm doing," Catherine argued. Ever since he was a child, Keith had been fastidious about following the rules. "These are church-sponsored programs," she said. "I'm just helping create a record of what is going on down there. Besides, it's not a matter of politics. It's a question of right and wrong."

"This obsession with doing good is a symptom of your grief," he argued. "Can't you see, this isn't your battle."

At last she said, "Look, I have to live with my loss. Gregory is gone. But Rosa's mother is undoubtedly alive. There is no earthly reason they should be separated any longer."

"That is no place for a woman like you," Father Pietro told her.

"That's the point," she said. "Women like me don't usually get involved in these matters, but I could help in this case. My late husband did business with most of the ruling families. I know important people there, people I've entertained over the years. One old friend owns a coffee plantation, I think it's near Rosa's village. He is one of the biggest land owners in the country; his brother is high up in the government. There are lots of Americans working for the church down there. You could arrange for me to get to the refugee camps near Rosa's mother. I could take down money, medical supplies they need. If I find Rosa's mother, I can pay to get her back here somehow."

"The people the church has sent are specially trained," Father Pietro said. "They understand the dangers and accept them as part of the lives they have chosen. You don't know what it is like down there. You don't have to go."

"But I want to. And if you don't help me I'll go anyway, on my own." She rolled the words from her tongue like a naughty child. She was fifty years old and starting into the world so late. Nothing could stop her, once she was determined. She told Keith that she was going first to Mexico City to revisit the places she had been with his father. It would help her come to grips with her loss. He made her promise she would keep an eye on developments in El Salvador and turn back "if the situation heated up."

At breakfast her waiter, who could not have been much older than Rosa, took her soft-boiled eggs to a corner table and shelled them before serving her, saving her the negligible pain of burning her hands on the hot shells.

She noticed an item in the newspaper with a San Salvador dateline. *"A cuatro campesinos . . .* four peasants . . . *les metieron unos palos . . .* stakes were driven *. . . por los oídos, la boca, y los ojos . . .* in their ears, mouth, eyes . . . *los quemaron vivos . . .* burned alive . . . " Feeling sick to the bone, she pushed away the remains of her breakfast and escaped to the darkness of her room.

Later that morning, she found a church near the hotel and lit a candle to Guadalupe for the four peasants. She knelt for a long time on the worn stone floor, drifting in a fever that had begun to flare through her at intervals. Then, even though she was feeling ill, she went with the bus tour to see the pyramids at Teotihuacán.

The bus wound its way through miles of slums and garbage dumps, a smoldering shantytown on the outskirts of the city. On higher ground, she gazed across the Valley of Mexico at the two snow-topped volcanoes. The starkness of the landscape—a plot of cultivated land with haystacks, a plot of corn, the flat blue sky streaked with cirrus clouds, patches of scrub pine—relieved the buzzing in her head. Colors which seemed garish to her in Mexican pottery and clothing were natural here, reflections of the land and sky. Stretched across the broad valley like massive outcroppings of stone were the remains of civilizations past: Tula, Cholula, Teotihuacán.

Gregory had never had the patience for bus travel; she wanted now to experience the country the way its people did. It was an indulgence to sit cushioned between two young mothers whose flesh seemed as warm and yielding as rising dough and watch the land unfold. When she stepped from the bus into the glare of high noon, a headache came like a blow, nearly blinding her with pain. She didn't feel like walking along these corridors with the scale of giants, the menacing Pathway of the Dead, but she forced herself. She had to see it all—the enormous platforms and temples and ball courts created centuries before for deadly games. Despite her headache, she climbed to the top of the Pyramid of the Sun. The guide pointed out the platform for the cutting of the heart from the body. He described the trajectory of the victim's corpse as it was flung down the steps. Catherine became dizzy. She had to sit on a step a third of the way down and wait until her head cleared. She could not bear the thought of a bleeding, still throbbing heart being pulled from behind that tight secure breastbone and the body cast away like so much garbage. She wanted to shut her ears, her eyes.

Here, tens of thousands had been offered to the fleshless jaws of death. Their skulls became playthings to be decorated with bits of obsidian and turquoise and displayed on racks. This was the place where the savage deities she had seen in Mexican art held sway: Coatlicue with her necklace of human hands and hearts, goggle-eyed Tlaloc, the god of rain, and most terrifying, Xipe Totec, the god of spring, whose priests wore the flayed skins of those who had been sacrificed.

She endured the bus ride back with eyes shut, head throbbing with pain. This is all part of the same thing, she thought.

The next morning the clock radio in Catherine's hotel room woke her with a jolt. "In San Salvador yesterday rooftop snipers firing submachine guns ambushed an anti-government march by some 150,000 leftists, leaving at least fifteen dead and ninety wounded, witnesses said."

Her fever was a continual thing, something she brushed aside like mosquitos in the jungle. It was a nuisance, but inevitable. She called her old friend Celestina in San Salvador to tell her she would be arriving there the next day.

"Come for an early dinner," Celestina said. "You will want to be back in your hotel before dark. Just a safety precaution, given the situation."

Catherine stayed in bed the rest of the day. In the early evening she dressed and took a taxi to the outskirts of the city, determined to see the Basilica of the Virgin of Guadalupe and the miraculous mantle of the Virgin, proof of her appearance to a peasant near that site. The old Basilica was sinking into the spongy lake beneath the city. One day it would join the great pyramids  below the surface. The new structure was modern, cool. Inside, she studied the display cases, translating the printed tags, but she could not find the mantle. At last she gave up and knelt in the back of the church for mass. Her knees pressed painfully against the floor. The young priest spoke in a monotone.

She was disappointed. She had hoped for a sign of some sort, that Guadalupe was with her, but the Virgin had let her down. She had wished for comfort as she faced this next step and found none. The tiny fissures of faith that had opened up inside her, the plant turning to the sun, pores open, shut again.

Back at the hotel, she asked the night clerk about the mantle. He told her it was over the altar. She had stared at it directly during mass and not seen it. She could imagine Gregory's reaction. Ever the skeptic, he would have teased her: "Plain as the nose on your face. You should have gone with a guide. But it's just like you, Cat, to go on your own, seeking a personal revelation."

Just before she drifted to sleep, she sensed his presence. He never would have approved of her trip. He would have said it was too dangerous. "Try to understand," she whispered. "It's my chance  to do something for someone else."

That night she dreamed of Guadalupe. Bloodstains bloomed on the Virgin's cloak like roses. Was this her sign?


Late the next afternoon, after an exhausting day of travel, Catherine took a taxi up into the hills overlooking the city of San Salvador to have dinner with Celestina. Over the years, the two of them had shopped together, lunched together, entertained each other. They had the sort of friendship forged by women whose husbands did business together.

Celestina was graying now, and still elegant. Her house was spacious, decorated in cream, beige and brown.

"Sergio will not be able to join us, he's in Madrid," she said. "We were so sorry to hear about Gregory. It must have been such a shock for you."

"He was always so healthy, we had no idea there was anything wrong with his heart. I miss him terribly."

"But let us not dwell on sadness. How was your flight?"

"Perfectly pleasant. But when I landed it was a surprise to see soldiers swarming all over the airport. And I got the third degree in customs. They wanted to know where I was going, who I was seeing. They went through everything—my luggage, the case of medical supplies I have with me for the center, down to the last bottle of aspirin. Do I look like a criminal?"

"You're bound to be noticed, and things are not normal."

"I've been following the troubles in the news, but even so it's a shock to feel how different it is from before."

"Come, let's eat." Celestina led her into a dining room where a white wrought iron and glass table was set with shrimp in aspic, papaya and pineapple, iced gazpacho, a frothy lemon pudding, tiny rolls.

"Forgive me if I don't eat much," Catherine said.

"Oh, it's all safe," Celestina said automatically. "Most of what we eat is imported from the States or France."

"I've been under the weather—nothing serious, the usual stomach upset."

"You should see my doctor."Celestina called for her maid to bring Catherine a tin of tiny white pills.

"Take these and promise me, if you are worse, if you begin to turn yellow, you will call my doctor. Here's his number, tell him I sent you. And where is it you are going next? I didn't quite understand your call."

"About an hour north of the capital."

Celestina frowned. "The countryside is not always safe these days. Do you have friends to take you there?"

"Not exactly. I will have someone to guide me, sent by the archdiocese. I'm taking money and medicine to a refugee camp the church runs there, and I hope to find the mother of the young girl I wrote you about. Her village is not far from where Sergio has a coffee farm, if I am correct."

"Yes, he does have some holdings there. He doesn't run them himself, you know. He never goes there. He doesn't know any of those people. I'm sorry, but he could not be helpful to you."

"I recall his brother is in the government. I was hoping he might be able to ask after her . . ."

"Oh, my dear, Sergio could not bring up the question of a peasant woman's whereabouts. It is beneath the attention of the ministers."

"But his brother—could he not inquire in some

informal manner? I love Rosa as if she were my daughter, and I am so eager to find her mother. I want to bring her back to California. I thought you and Sergio could help. I counted on it, in fact."

Celestina sat forward in her chair. "You must stop this. Are you crazy? You want to bring this woman back to the States with you? Who is this woman? What has she done that you need to take her away like this?"

"She has done nothing wrong. Her son was murdered last fall and she sent Rosa north and now I want to bring them back together."

"Catherine, I can only tell you that you have been misinformed about what happens here. You must be careful not to become the plaything of the rebels. You say you are visiting a center run by the church?"

"That's right. The archdiocese in San Francisco made the arrangements."

"And this is what you told the men in customs?"

"Yes. What's wrong with that?"

"When you say 'church' in California, it has one meaning. It sometimes has a different meaning here. In El Salvador, Guatemala, and before, in Nicaragua, the church is helping the campesinos. Is that what you have heard?"

"Yes, the peasants."

"But the campesinos, the Indians, they are rebels. It is in the blood. They want to make trouble."

"Is that what you think is happening here?"

"The campesinos want to take over the land, don't they? It's the same all over Latin America. There have been rebels in the mountains for centuries. They are being armed and trained by the Cubans, the Nicaraguans. They are coming into the cities. If it weren't for the military here, good people like you and me could not sleep easily. Why do you think we have electrified walls around this house? They would slaughter us in our sleep, believe me."

"I can't ignore what I've seen with my own eyes. I've met people who have been tortured, I've seen their scars."

"I think you should go back to California, my friend. Sergio can make arrangements for you to return quickly. I know he would be happy to help."

"I'm not going back until I do what I came to do. I'm disappointed you won't make it easier."

"If you stay, I can't say Sergio can help you if you run into trouble. These are difficult times for all of us. No one is above reproach. I beg you, leave this business to us. Gregory would have understood that was the proper thing to do."

"You're right. Gregory never got involved in a country's domestic affairs. He always had to think of the bank's position. I represent no one but myself."

"I see you are unshakeable." Celestina sighed. "You always were a stubborn one. But if you change your mind, please call us."


Back at the hotel Catherine collected a message from the clerk. Father Sebastián would pick her up at 9 a.m. in the lobby. She spent several hours calling old friends, explaining about Rosa's mother, but she got nowhere. Polite conversation, condolences over Gregory, would like to help but. She had assumed that Celestina and Sergio would help, or one of the others. Gregory had extended so many professional courtesies over the years. College admissions for their sons, designer dresses for their daughters, visits with governors, congressmen, generals. Without him, she had no power.

She lay awake most of the night in her hotel room. Her conversation with Celestina had sinister undertones. There was some logic to this place she did not understand. She tried to focus through her tension and fever, to understand the danger here. She felt it like the pulse in her throat. Terrible things happened to people. Celestina's life went on as normal. She was here of her own choice, but she had not understood how high the stakes might be. For the first time, she wrestled with an impulse to go home.


Father Sebastián, a Salvadoran priest a few years younger than Keith, and a shy seventeen-year-old driver came for Catherine the next morning. Both wore chinos, striped polo shirts and running shoes. Father Sebastian was lean and athletic, with wavy brown hair and a full mustache. Rodolfo was chunky and strong through the upper body. He kept his eyes on the priest, as if waiting for cues, and never looked at her directly.

Father Sebastian's English was excellent. He had been trained in Westchester county, he explained, then spent a few months at a parish in Brooklyn. He had good news for her: they had found Rosa's mother. "We'll take you to her," he said. "Her village has been the center of fighting. You know how it goes. The rebels hold it for awhile, then the army. It's nearly deserted now. But we found a cousin who said she had gone to a nearby village and told us how to reach her. I know the area—it's near where I grew up. We'll take a side trip to find her on the way to the center."

They were driving on a narrow unpaved road through a pine forest. The sky was blue, the air deliciously cool. The coffee farms below were visible at intervals, patches of deep green as they came to curves along the mountain.

Catherine began to relax. Everything was going to work out. Her fears of the night before seemed silly in the sunlight. Her mind raced ahead to the next few days. She would meet Rosa's mother and deliver her case of supplies to the refugee camp. If Rosa's mother was willing to come back with her, she would renew her efforts to arrange it, try the American embassy. Surely it would all be possible.

Fever sent small waves up her back and she shivered from time to time, but the sensation was almost pleasant.

"Are you all right?" Father Sebastián asked. "You are so pale."

"It's nothing serious, just a stomach bug," she said.

"Don't take it lightly. There are diseases here you don't have in the States."

"Have you ever thought of living there?" she asked him.

"This is where I belong," he said. He told her of his childhood in these mountains, his call to the priesthood, his commitment to helping the people who were his relatives and neighbors.

He went silent and scanned the road ahead. At first she didn't see the van. It was parked in the shadow. It was the sort of van Keith and his friends took into the mountains when they went camping. She could hear Gregory's voice: Plain as the nose on your face.

Father Sebastián gripped Rodolfo's shoulder. "Watch out," he said in a low voice. The van was moving, angling into the center of the road, blocking their way.

"Someone must be having car trouble," Catherine said as Rodolfo braked to a stop.

Four men walked toward them from the shadowed side of the road. They were young and slim and wore khaki uniforms and dark sunglasses and carried guns.

"*Buenos diás*," the leader said with exaggerated politeness. "We have some questions for our friend the Padre." He opened the back door and pulled Father Sebastián out by the arm.

"And who is this?" he continued. "A visitor? We must make her welcome."

"Don't worry," Father Sebastián said softly. "This is just a game they play." She allowed the man to help her from the car. If Gregory were here, they wouldn't frighten me, she thought. He would know what to do to take care of them.

The man took off his sunglasses. When she saw his eyes she knew terror. No. It was the same feeling she had when she saw Gregory lifeless in the hospital. Her head began to throb. The man put his sunglasses in his shirt pocket. His expression was as artificial as a mask. He smelled of sweat. She saw the rows of bullets across his chest and tried to say something, but she found she could not speak.

"Come, you must not make us wait," he said, nudging her with his shoulder. He was only a few inches taller than she was. The other three men clustered around Father Sebastián and Rodolfo and pushed at them roughly.

The men were leading them down a dim pathway in the forest. Catherine stumbled over the roots of trees and large stones in a daze of fear. She heard a commotion and turned. Rodolfo had bolted. Before she could understand, two of the men had shot him in the back many times. His body flew in a grotesque cartwheel and landed face up in the knotted roots of a tree, his body twisted, his eyes staring at the sliver of sky above.

Catherine screamed and started back toward him. The leader gripped her by the arm. "Oh, have we frightened our friend? What a shame. She should see the condition of the men they blew up this morning. Not a pretty sight."

They came to a small clearing. The leader said, "*Con permiso*," and slid one leg behind Catherine and shoved. She hit the ground hard. Time slowed and she felt her body pulse with the fuel of her panic.

As she lay on her back, her head twisted sideways, she saw the other men surround Father Sebastián and tear off his shirt. They were talking so fast she could hardly understand. She heard something about an ambush. The rebels had ambushed the soldiers somewhere nearby. They thought he was involved? He had been through here several days before? Father Sebastián was shaking his head.

One of the men kicked him between the legs, hit him in the mouth, then pulled him up and hit him hard under the ribs. He was bleeding now. Catherine screamed at them to stop. "He's just a boy," she said stupidly.

The leader held a pistol to her head and forced her to watch as they tortured Father Sebastián with bayonets.

"See, this is what we do to communists," he said. "Are these your friends? Tell me, are you one of these? A nice lady like you?"

Catherine forced herself to focus. "I am no communist. What makes you think he is? Make them stop. This is enough. Make them stop now."

"In the United States, they do not treat communists this way? Ah, what a civilized country. Here we are primitive. But we think our methods work. You will see. We won't have any more trouble with him when we're through. No, don't shut your eyes." He dug the end of the pistol into her temple.

She retched and he pressed her head against the ground in her own sour smell.

Father Sebastián was reciting the rosary in a tight, faint voice, as if the words were being ripped from his throat. He was covered with blood, and the earth around him was dark with it.

If I ever get out of here, Catherine thought in a surge of helpless fury, I will not stop until I have made these men pay for what they are doing.

"Now," the leader said. Suddenly he came down upon her and pulled her clothes away. She pounded against his chest with her fists and howled with outrage. One of the others hit her in the head with the butt of his gun until she was dizzied and bleeding and stopped fighting. She dug her fingernails into the dirt and tried to block out the pain.

Help me, Guadalupe, she prayed. I can't bear it.

She heard gunshots. Father Sebastián cried out one last time. She was next. These could be her last moments, the murderous stranger intruding upon her body her last human contact. Nothing could save her.

She smelled cigarette smoke. There was a roaring in her ears and the sound of laughter as the men joked among themselves.

Only now, as she approached the end of hope, could she sense Guadalupe's presence. Please help me, she prayed. A strange silence came upon her. She pulled herself into a piercing instant: Guadalupe with her gentle downcast face with its trail of tears, the Virgin with the bloodstained mantle, could not make the suffering stop. She was helpless against the habit of evil. She had no power here. Nothing could help.

The man fell hard upon her. Take me, Guadalupe, she murmured. The weapons made the sounds of preparation. There was an ungodly roar, and she moved at last beyond the borders of pain.

Sometimes when she drifted out of her drugged darkness into the stark white hospital room she saw a priest, a black-haired stocky man her own age with dignified carriage. He stood at the window looking out, or in the doorway looking in on her, but never came close enough for her to see him clearly. As she slid in and out of awareness she believed she was in a nightmare, but the stabs of pain in her body told her it was real.

There were doctors here in the nightmare and a nurse who told her stories: They were all dead. Rodolfo. Father Sebastián. All the people in the village near the rebel ambush had been massacred. She had been left for dead but, miraculously, she had survived. A peasant on a shortcut through the woods had found her and noticed she was still breathing and brought her to the hospital in a pickup truck loaded with hay. She was dusty and bleeding from a bullet through the top of her head, and also . . . well, you know what happened.

"Yes," Catherine said, speaking for the first time. "I know." The nurse wanted to know her name, and what she was doing here. Catherine tried to answer. As she lay there she saw a kaleidescope of images, the pattern of her life telescoped and fragmented, in an intense starburst: Gregory. Keith. Father Pietro. Rosa. Father Sebastián. Guadalupe.

"Rosa's mother," she said. Then she understood that she, too, was dead in that village. Tears streamed down her face and she sobbed until the nurse brought back the darkness with the stab of a needle.

She came awake again, alone, and saw a tiny statue of Guadalupe set into the wall near her bed. The Virgin was modeled in plaster, with pretty touches of azure and gilt. She had faded now for Catherine, like an object once beloved in childhood that when contemplated evokes strong memories of devotion but not the emotion itself.

She had to get home to Rosa. When the nurse came she gave her name, and asked her to contact Keith and someone from the American embassy and someone from the refugee center. She refused the painkillers so she could think clearly.

Miraculously, she had survived. But why? She stared at the impassive face of Guadalupe.

It was impossible for her to comprehend the core of faith she had sensed in Father Sebastián. She had started out months before to regain her own faith. She had tried, but she had not. Perhaps it was impossible for a woman from her background to believe in the same way he did. Perhaps there were too many layers of comfort and skepticism between the raw experience of living and the apprehension of the holy for her to feel the presence of God. But in lieu of faith she had been given something else . . . what? Some new sort of understanding? Knowledge of some sort of truth?

"Someone has to do something," she said when Keith arrived, stricken, at her bedside.

"Enough," he cried angrily. "Isn't this enough, what happened to you?"

"What happened is my own fault. A priest and a young man are dead. I made a mistake. It's too late for them, but somebody has to do something about it."

"You have waltzed down here into a civil war, don't you understand?" Keith said. "Now everyone wants to know what you were doing here. The embassy has had calls from Washington. Their man is a saint, but Washington wants this cleared up fast, and he wants you back home." He was white with anger, the way Gregory used to be when things were out of his control. Now that Keith was in his thirties he looked more and more like Gregory, with his gray eyes and firm demeanor. She wasn't about to let him confuse her.

"You know what I was doing here. Tell them."

There were other visitors, too. The ambassador. Celestina, Sister Mary Joseph from the refugee center, even Sergio. They kept up a steady murmuring. Such a horrible thing. A tragedy. In the wrong place at the wrong time. Celestina and Keith were telling each other the story of the misdirected American, a recent widow, setting out against their advice to wander into a place where she did not belong. She didn't know what she was getting into. She should have stayed in California.

She wanted to scream at them, save your pity for those who really need it. I'm an imposter. What happened to me is nothing, a drop of water in an ocean of violence.

She was angry at herself. How could she have thought she could do any good by being here? She was eager to see Guadalupe's miraculous mantle, eager to offer Rosa's mother the comfort of her own privilege, how could she not have recognized her own arrogance?

One morning she asked the nurse about the priest she had seen. "Yes, the archbishop was here many times. He wants to talk with you."

And so he came.

"I have been foolish," she said when he sat at her bedside, close enough for her to see his weariness. She began to weep. He made no move to comfort her. She yearned to confess her pride, her guilt, her blind vanity.

"I'm responsible for Father Sebastián's death," she said. "If he had not been helping me, he'd still be alive."

"He was where he wanted to be, with or without you. He knew the risks. We all do. You didn't have to come here, you didn't have to suffer this way. But suffering is not an end in itself."

"I was trying to do something, some little thing to help . . ."

"Who knows what God has in mind for you."

He rose from the chair and went to stare out the window. She waited, sensing that something had to pass between them.

"You should go home soon. You may be in danger if you stay."

"Why?"

He sighed. He was impatient with her.

"You are a witness. You saw their faces, what they did. You have the power of an American citizen, and believe me, that is more than any Salvadoran in your position could muster. Of course, they could try to discredit you . . ."

"They . . . ?"

He ignored her interruption. "But you may be strong enough to make your story believed under the harshest scrutiny. Perhaps you have something to carry you through . . . a strong faith?"

His dark eyes studied her, as if trying to fathom this foreign creature, this woman whose life paralleled his in history but was so removed in circumstance.

She was shaken by his intensity, but she had to tell the truth.

"I cannot share the faith of those I have seen here." She told him about her devotion to Guadalupe, about her wish to do something after Gregory's death, her love for Rosa. She described what happened in the clearing. She opened her heart to him. She had tried, and her intentions were good, and she had encountered brutality beyond imagining, but she had to face her own limitations now. "Compared to you, I am dead inside," she said, and then she added, vehemently, "But something has to be done. Those men should be punished."

"Is there anything you can believe in?" he inquired gently.

"Justice . . . Right and wrong. Mercy." She said the words without thinking. He nodded his head, as if satisfied.

"Use that, then. And use your anger. Go home now. Get well. Then tell what you know. Tell the truth of what you have seen, what you have experienced. That is enough."

He bowed his head and sat at her side for a long time, and she felt in his silent presence a forgiveness of all the weaknesses she had confessed to him.

When he left she settled back against the pillows feeling a sense of confirmation. The tightness in her chest, that mixture of pride, anguish, grief and confusion, knotted there so long she had felt it as part of her breathing, melted away. She knew what to do next. He had shown her the way.

# THE ALMOST-PERFECT MAN

SALLY WAS RUNNING in the Berkeley hills just after sunrise on the longest day of the year. She was thinking about the hours of daylight stretched out before her. Here at midsummer was an expanded, special day when sunshine rendered each detail sharp and spilled over into the evening. Even this early, it dazzled her. In the stillness she was aware of the piercing smell of eucalyptus, the brittleness of the drying grass along the path, the steady working of her heart, the sweat as it trickled down the small of her back. Breathing hard, just on the edge of pain, she felt a physical joy so intense and pure, she wished it were a tangible thing— a stone, a shell, a piece of weathered wood—to carry home with her.

As she neared thirty-five, she wanted more than ever to feel the vitality of her body, to use it. She ran twenty-five miles a week. For the first time in her life her thighs were taut, legs trim, and she was brown from the sun. Aha, she thought. Who says eighteen is better?

In the final blocks of her run, moving back into city streets, she was jarred by the concrete sidewalks, the car exhaust that lingered in the air, the bedraggled scavengers who made a permanent home on Telegraph Avenue. She slowed her pace as she approached the Pendragon Cafe. Cappuccino and *pain au chocolate* were Sally's way of rewarding herself for her efforts. Roger always heated the pastry for her until the chocolate melted into the buttery layers. This morning, he waved and called out, "Cappuccino coming up," as she walked past him and settled into her favorite seat near the back. From there she could hear Roger handle three conversations and half a dozen drink orders at once. Some days it was as speedy as a fast game of tennis.

Roger was a scholar, he was a clown. He knew all the daily baseball scores and the schedule of movies at the Pacific Film Archive by heart. He tossed off one-liners while bussing the tables, and burst into snatches of Broadway tunes while cleaning the espresso machine. The cafe was his living room and his stage. At holidays he gathered a dozen or so regulars for elaborate meals he cooked himself, creating a family.

Last year Roger had asked Sally to join them for Thanksgiving. Both of her parents were dead; she hadn't been back to Manchester in years. He had served roast duck, wild rice, baked squash,three kinds of pie, and lots of wine. He had asked her to stay on after the others had left, and they had made love for the first time.

Sally liked everything about Roger. She liked his fast wit and his dandelion curls, his wiry build and his ease with women—a fact he credited to having two sisters. But that Thanksgiving night she had felt guarded despite the wine and after-dinner Calvados. Roger was more awkward than she would have guessed. And she had not found with him the sexual spark, the mysterious physical urge, that she had felt with other, less likable men. She had tried, in the months that followed, to manufacture passion for him, but each of them realized it was not going to happen.

"Let's just go with it," Roger said.

So despite what he referred to as "the missing link," they were steady companions—a couple. They buffered each other against loneliness and slept together sometimes, in a friendly way. Sally called him "the almost-perfect man for me."

"You're out running early today," Roger said as he brought her cappuccino and sat opposite her.

"I started at six, while it was still cool. Even so, I was dripping by the end. I haven't felt this sort of heat since I was a kid in the East. I thought Northern California was the land of no extremes."

"Well, this is supposed to be a record heat wave, and today is shaping up to be another scorcher. Global warming. It's driving people nuts. This morning right after I opened up, a women came in and ordered an iced soy latte. I took it over to her, she took one sip and threw it in my face. 'I didn't ask for cinnamon,' she said. I was furious. And I see so many crazies I can't tell anymore which ones are dangerous."

"You're too nice. People take advantage of you." She smiled and gave his hand a squeeze. He was wearing his Yankees t-shirt and faded blue jeans, a white dishtowel around his narrow waist.

"I'm a nice guy, sure, but I can't take much more of this. I need a break. Why don't we go down to Baja?"

"Talk about hot!"

"Yeah, but down there they know how to do it. We could lie around and drink Margaritas. No worries."

"I can't. I have a Virginia Woolf seminar to teach during summer session, which starts next week. The dean called me yesterday and asked me to fill in for Barnstead. His grant came through and he's off to London on Friday. So I have to spend the next few days preparing. I started rereading *The Waves* last night."

"Ah . . . 'Death is the enemy,'" Roger intoned, going down to one knee and tilting his face upward. "Against you I will fling myself, unvanquished and unyielding, O Death!'" He slumped forward, clutching his throat.

"Bravo!" Sally said. "I don't know how you can remember so much. My own memory seems to be failing. On the other hand, I understand more. Every sentence in that book says, 'Time is passing.' I didn't notice that when I read it as an undergraduate."

"My favorite professor in graduate school at Columbia used to say *The Waves* was like a dance," Roger said. "The characters move in and out of a pattern but they never connect." He stood. "Another cappuccino? The second is on the house, solstice special."

"Thanks, no. I don't want to get too wired. I'm going to spend the rest of the day in bed, behind drawn curtains, sweating into my pillow and reading."

"I have to stay open an extra hour for a staff meeting, but I'll be by around nine, if you want. We could blow on each other or something."

"See you then."


The telephone rang shortly after four o'clock as Sally lay in bed reading.

"Sally? You're still there. I wasn't sure."

She recognized the accent at once. "Stefan? Are you in California?"

"No, in Warsaw."

The phone line crackled. She pictured the globe spinning.They were talking after a silence of nearly eight years, connected by a fragile thread of impulses beamed off a satellite.His call was as disconcerting as if he had arrived on her front doorstep unannounced.

"What time is it there?" she asked. It was a stupid question, she realized at once, but it bought her time to calm down. Together they computed the distance in time zones. Nine hours. As bright as it was outside her window, in Warsaw it was deepest night.

"You're almost forty now," she said.

"And you're thirty-two."

"A younger woman." It was a familiar exchange.

"How are your children?"

"Fine."

"How old are they getting to be?" She remembered the two birth announcements, formally engraved, and the colorful foreign postage, but not their names. A boy and a girl. The first one had arrived less than a year after Stefan had left her.

"Marta is five, Kurt is three," he said.

They shared news of their accomplishments. He had published a collection of his reports from Bosnia. She had been granted tenure at the university.He had been in Rome for the past year, covering the Vatican, and was on his way to Bangkok to do an update on the Golden Triangle. She was writing a book on the image of the woman artist in nineteenth-century British literature.

She wondered what he looked like now, but didn't know how to ask. When she had known him in graduate school, his fair hair had been long, and he had a light down of hair on his chest and arms. His skin was rosy. She had met him during the fall quarter after he had gone to the Ethiopia to help distribute famine relief. He was passionate about human rights, and seemed to have more faith in human nature than she did. Together they had gone to dozens of conferences and workshops. In their few classes together he was the challenger, she the scholar. In bed he was tender and thoughtful. Remembering now, she felt a surge of yearning. She wanted to say, "Stefan, we're not so young any more. I don't care as much about anything. Has that happened to you?"

Stefan was the first lover who wanted to know what she thought about the books they were reading, the end of the Cold War, the state of relations between men and women. He talked to her like an intimate friend, but he never once said he loved her. If she had married him . . . but he had never asked, and she had never ventured to bring it up. He told her that Polish men prided themselves on being independent. She assumed he never would marry. When he completed his master's degree in political science he returned to Warsaw, to the newspaper job that was waiting. She drove him to the airport and hid her tears.

When the first birth announcement arrived and she realized he had married almost at once, she had exhausted herself with furious weeping. Gradually her vision of him faded.

Even now Stefan was the only one who shared the secret of the child they had conceived, the child she mourned every year on the imagined birthday. If she had known at twenty-six that she could not be a mother by thirty-two, she might have had the baby. She might have thrown a scene and forced him to marry her. But the pregnancy was frightening. She felt betrayed by her body, out of control. Although Stefan was solicitous when she was ill in the mornings before class, he insisted that the time was not right for either of them to become parents. He had not begun his career, nor had she. They could not take on the obligation of a child, he said. At last she had agreed with his reasoning. She allowed him to find her a safe doctor, to drive her to the office one bright summer day. He waited while she went through the tugging pain, and held her while she wept when it was over.

"Alice and I are divorced," Stefan was saying now. "It happened last year. We share the children, fifty-fifty. I'm meeting her in San Francisco next month." He would be coming from Warsaw, his former wife from New York, where she had spent the past six months as a translator at the United Nations. Sally imagined his plane taking off and landing, Alice and the children in midair. She pictured all of them blonde and blue-eyed like he was. They were a modern family, popping in and out of airplanes as casually as some people hailed taxicabs.

"And I can come over to Berkeley after I collect them," he said. "I want to see my old haunts. I want to see you."

"No, I'll be away," she lied, feeling panic. "I'm going to Mexico with a friend."

"When will you be back? I can stay around for a few days."

"Not until September."

"I really want to see you, Sally. I always thought I made a mistake, not staying with you."

"Why are you telling me this now?" Suddenly she was filled with anger. "You never brought it up before, not even when I was pregnant."

"I was afraid. We were so young."

"That didn't stop you from marrying Alice."

"I wasn't ready. I wasn't sure I'd get to do what I wanted to do. It was easier to take care of it that way."

"Easier for you."

"And you? You wouldn't have been able to finish your doctorate, to take a full-time teaching job."

"Who's to say? Maybe I could have done it all. Maybe it would have taken longer. No one can know how it would have been."

What right did he have to call her and bring it all back again?

"Then you come see me," he was saying. "Or I'll meet you halfway. In London, or Amsterdam. New York. Wherever you say."

"No, Stefan."

"I can't persuade you?"

"Not this time."

"If you change your mind, call me. I'll be here. Let me give you the number . . ."

"You don't understand," she interrupted. "I don't want to see you again. It's too late." She broke the connection and lay back, feeling drained by unexpected emotion.

Hanging on the wall across from her bed was the weaving Stefan had bought for her in Mendocino as a reward for passing her orals. It was shaped like a circle, with green and brown bands at the bottom, a narrow strip of azure at the top. It was called "Earth and Air." It was a touchstone for a time in her life when she had felt both grounded and inspired. In those dreamy graduate-school years, she had thought a lot about achieving equilibrium, a perfect balance. Yin and yang. With Stefan she was complete, woman and thinker. She gazed at the weaving. After getting over Stefan she had thought of herself as full of potential, unattached. Now it occurred to her that she might instead be empty, floating aimlessly—or she might be earthbound, hampered by her own lack of imagination.

Stefan had chosen marriage, children, the work he wanted. She had settled for only part of what could have been. Now she wondered if the pain he had caused her had closed her off in some way. She supposed she had measured each potential lover against a vision of Stefan, the ideal partner, and their fantasy child—a shadow family, abstract and perfected.

While she was with Stefan, she never believed he would leave her. But he did. And now he had left Alice too. She doubted that he saw any connection between the two of them, yet for a moment she could see herself as one of two interchangeable women, arbitrarily placed in time. She wondered why he had never asked her to come to Warsaw. She wondered if he had ever told Alice he loved her, and if she had believed him.

Late-afternoon sunlight slipped throught the Venetian blinds and dappled the bedroom wall with lozenges of burning light. The weaving seemed stale to her now, distasteful. Tomorrow she would take it down. The room was stifling. She felt short of breath, painfully self-enclosed. She sensed for the first time an emptiness beyond imagining. There were limits to be encountered soon, unexpected barriers.

Stefan had flitted around the world, settling here, settling there. She had stayed behind. He had opened her up in so many ways, excited her, but he had never loved her in a steady, devoted way.And he had never expected to stay. After he left, she tended to stick with familiar people and places, saving the unknown for next month, next year. She was rooted now. But what next?

What if she were to conceive today? June, July, August . . . a March baby. She might have a spirited daughter. What would her coloring be? The shape of her eyes, nose, mouth, hands? Sally herself could not sing, could not paint. She never would be a whiz at math, like her brother Ian, or a trailblazing reporter, like Stefan. But a child could carry her beyond her own limits, connect her with some point in the future.

She pictured Roger holding her daughter, throwing her up in the air. The baby chuckled and held her arms out to him. She had dandelion curls and big brown eyes. Sally could imagine Roger as a funny, loving father. She began to wonder what it would be like to live with him day by day, without the shadow of Stefan behind him. She was able to think of other possibilities, as well. There was still time, she thought as she lay daydreaming.

Later, when she heard Roger's key in the front door lock, she felt a new sense of anticipation.

"Are you asleep?" he whispered as he came to sit beside her.

"No," she whispered back. "I'm awake now."

# GRIDLOCK

THERE IS A photograph of Niagara Falls on the giant Kodak sign in the main concourse of Grand Central Station today. I see Niagara and think, Honeymoon. One week there was an image of the royal couple, Bonnie Charlie and Lady Di, in the royal carriage, galloping headlong into marriage. When I saw it I wondered, did Pico and I look that innocent and rosy when we took a cab to City Hall nearly ten years ago? I supposed we did, but things certainly haven't turned out as I'd expected.

I stand for a moment under the great starry dome of the station and look at the silvery-blue water of the Falls trapped within the photographer's rectangular frame, crystallized on the edge of action. I can almost hear the roar the water makes, thundering over its course.

I'm on my way home after a rehearsal of the play I'm in, rushing through Grand Central toward the 104 bus stop. From the side room off Forty-second Street, a woman's voice stops me cold. I can pinpoint her location within seconds. She sits in a phone booth along the wall, spilling rage into the glass cubicle and bouncing it from the ceiling, whipping the syllables off the concrete with the punch of a tennis player. The anger in her voice strikes the ears of hundreds of people, assaulting us with unmistakable heat, arousing in each a pinprick of guilt, fear, sympathy or reciprocal rage.

Looks of shock and embarrassment sweep through the crowd. The vendors glance in her direction as they dish out change to the commuters buying their newspapers. The men slouching near the Off-Track Betting booth turn their eyes warily toward the exit and draw themselves into a fight-or-flight stance. Commuters step up their pace a beat or two at the hint of danger.

What a performance! A few years back, before I got my big break, I would have envied her the power to create this effect.

The woman is well-dressed in a dove-gray suit. Her hair is dark, pulled back into a knot with tendrils floating, Ophelia-like, alongside her ears. She doesn't look like a loony or a babbler. It is impossible to tell what might have brought her to this point.

Probably a man. I've been that angry with Pico at times.

I married Pico because I wanted passion in my life, not safety. I met him when I was a senior at the High School for the Performing Arts. He was five years older than I and already a working actor. People think Pico is Puerto Rican, but he's not. He's Cuban. His family left when Castro took over. His father had been a doctor; in this country he was retrained to be a reference librarian. Pico grew up with servants. His family is very cultured; unlike my maternal forbears, who fled the potato famine in Ireland, they considered their life in this country a definite comedown. But the parts Pico plays are at the other end of the scale: street toughs, petty drug dealers, pimps, junkies and convicts. Over the year he has had to toughen up a lot, just to keep in shape for his roles. He's done everything but go on the needle to prepare for parts. At times it's like living with a lunatic. Early on, I made myself a promise: If he's ever cast as a murderer, I'm moving out.

After we married I spent five years going out on casting calls. I tried for television commercials, walk-ons, bit parts, the soaps, anything. I was good, my acting coach said, but I didn't stand out. I had a few Off Broadway parts but made no money to speak of. Finally Pico pointed out that we needed two incomes to live in New York, so I got a job at a restaurant on Columbus Avenue. I had the four o'clock to midnight shift. Compared to what I was used to, the pay was good and the tips were better. I played the waitress to the hilt. But the combination of my hours and Pico's hours cut back on our love life. And Pico began to change, as well.

In the early years of our marriage he couldn't get enough of me. I was his juicy plum. He was my magic man, my seed-spilling hugger lover. Oh, we would go at it. Then one night he said, "Keep it on," when I began to slink my nightgown off over my head. Another night he said, "Don't you have any other clothes? I come home, you're always wearing the same old thing." He didn't even smile to show me he was kidding, the way he usually did.

I'd heard there could be points like this in a marriage, but I didn't think it would ever happen to us. I figured it was my fault. I took a little money I had set aside and joined a health club. I saw it as an investment in my future. I was holding onto my man.

After six months with the weight-training machines, I was lean as could be. You think he appreciated it? No way. Muscles turned him off, he said. He didn't like lady jocks.

But I liked the way I felt. When I buttoned my blouse after a session at the gym, my skin felt warm and smooth from the steam and my blood vessels tingled. When I breathed deeply I was aware of the bands of muscles beneath my breasts, the intricate webbing along my ribcage. I could open the doors in buses wide with one arm, full range of motion. I enjoyed the ripples of power. I was amazed at the hardness of my upper arms. They could have belonged to someone else—a woman who could swim the English Channel, a woman who could play at Wimbledon, a woman who could defend herself.

The better I felt, the less Pico seemed to enjoy me. Oh, there were still nights when he turned to me with the old passion, but they were fewer and fewer. For me there was no turning back. We had hit a real dead spot in our lives together. Gridlock. Like the dreaded point when all streams of traffic come to a grinding halt. I'd never felt so hateful toward Pico. Angry. Cold. Don't tread on me. And he began to give me the silent treatment. One day I said, "Let's call a truce." And he said, "Baby, I don't even recognize your existence." He spoke out of the corner of his mouth. I wasn't even sure it was me he was talking to. He was getting ready to play a hit man Off Off Broadway. And I couldn't afford to leave him. Which brings me to our rent-controlled apartment.

The apartment had been in Pico's family fifteen years when we moved in. His mother had died and his father moved to Miami to live with his sister, and it was ours. The building was constructed in the early part of the century for a style of life few of us can manage today. We have eight rooms, and pay only three hundred dollars a month.

Let me take you on a Circle Line tour of the place. The wall on your left is covered with stills from every play and movie Pico has been in since he started out in *West Side Story*. (He couldn't dance but he looked the part of a Shark, so they taught him enough to get by.) Ever since that first role he has paraded around in wise-guy t-shirts and headbands and zoot suits and black leather jackets and prison jumpsuits, getting into character. When he plays junkies he goes on a juice fast to drop ten pounds. Poor Pico. When he's working, he's not himself. When he's between parts and hustling, he doesn't know who he is. No wonder we've had troubles.

That lamp was once owned by Sal Mineo, an early idol of ours. Pico saw *Rebel Without a Cause* at an impressionable age.

This cigarette burn on the carpet occurred during a night when six of us drank a gallon of red wine and ate three pounds of pasta and did a marathon reading of *Cat on a Hot Tin Roof*. After the other couples left, Pico made love to me longer and harder than he ever had before. It happened in that very spot. Neither of us could walk. Later he lit a cigarette and fell asleep. I caught it just in time.

Pico has been a chain smoker ever since I've known him. It has stained his teeth and the skin on the insides of his palms. He smokes mainly Gauloises, cupping them between finger and thumb, the way an old con taught him once when he was playing an armed robber. Sometimes he blows the smoke in my face. His hot, fierce breath sends chills down my spine.

Here, in the kitchen, this crack in the plaster signifies the night I winged a plate at Pico in an argument about whether or not there was anything left between us. I had taken the position that there was not, but that I still believed the potential existed if he would try. He was taking the position that it didn't make any difference to him one way or another. Curiously, after I threw the plate, shattering it behind his head within inches of his pale, vulnerable neck, he was nicer to me for a week.

This coffee table is on loan from my friend Ingrid. Ingrid is a charter member of Demands on the World, Unlimited. Her therapist lives nearby, and three times a week she drops by for a post-session wrap-up. Ingrid's neurosis is as palpable as a deformity of the spine. Sometimes I think I could run my fingertips along it and feel the obstruction, a mass of primary experience distorted, congealed. From the time her father left her, when she was three, to the present, Ingrid's men have treated her poorly. It's hard to believe a woman with her looks—she's a blooming six-foot Nordic beauty—could have been seduced and abandoned so many times. Before they erupt into ugliness, her men treat her to trips to the Bahamas in winter, to the races at Saratoga in summer, to the Cape for autumn weekends, to Aspen, to Banff, to Cannes and Cancun. Oh, how I envy her those trips. I vacillate between sympathy and exasperation as I tune in to her stories.

For a long time I kept my own counsel about my problems with Pico. Then one afternoon I told her I was afraid he had lost interest in me. "I don't know what to do," I said. "It's been nearly two weeks since he's come near me . . . ."

"Mmmm," Ingrid said with a faraway look in her eyes. I waited, wishing I could retract my confession.

Then she told me a story about something that had happened to her at work that day. She does public relations for a senior citizens' group.

"This morning," she said, "after the workshop, a group of us were waiting for a bus. Two of my old men rushed when it came. One of them tripped on a slippery spot in the street. He threw his arm out as he fell and linked elbows by accident with the other. They flew into the air together, like they were dancing. There they were, two old men tumbling about, hats and beards flying. It was like a Chagall painting. Then bam, they were lying on the street. I went to help them up but an old woman held me back. 'Don't,' she said. 'You'll embarrass them.' So I just stood and waited.

"There was a third old man close to them. After they were on their feet again, breathing hard, their eyes wavering and tearing, you know what he said? 'Shouldn't have been rushing.'" Ingrid let out a snort of irritation. "What makes people do that? He saw the shock they felt at being off balance. 'Shouldn't have done that.' I felt like slapping him."

"What are you trying to tell me?"

"Well, you seem off balance, too. Topsy turvy. I'm not crazy about Pico, but there must be reasons why you stay with him. From the outside I see you stumbling, but I'm not going to tell you, 'Shouldn't have married him, shouldn't have done that.'"

She was right. There are lots of reasons why I stay with Pico. At times he's made me happier than any other human being has, for one. From the time he let me come watch from the wings as an awestruck eighteen-year-old I've been excited by his presence on stage, no matter what the part. My passion for him I've already covered. And I've always had a loyal streak. Which is not to say I didn't suffer greatly from hunger of the skin when he began giving me the cold shoulder. But when I found my gaze dwelling upon shapely forearms and haunches, upon young bodies arched at barres along upper Broadway at dusk, upon teenage boys with creamy skin and light down on their arms and new muscles rippling at ribs and backbones, when I found myself watching the men at the gym as we sweated together, breathing in on the upswings, out on the downswings, it was always Pico I wanted.

After my talk with Ingrid, I began to balance all the good years against half a dozen bad months and to hope that something would change.

This is our bedroom. Outside this window you can hear Floria. I call her the lovebird. She sends her cries into the air outside our bedroom window virtually every night. She sits in her apartment on the tenth floor like a tropical bird perched high in a palm tree, chattering into the breeze. Released from the restraints of the state when they emptied the mental institutions, she made herself available to all. The men stand outside on the street in the midnight hours and whistle. "Floria? Oh, Floria." Their voices caress the syllables; their tongues roll, juicy with anticipation. "Flo-ria . . . Flo-ree-a . . . Flori-aaaaa." Her response drifts down, with laughter and intimations of the pleasures to come.

Last summer, at the height of our gridlock period, I thought I would go crazy listening to Floria, with her Caribbean rhythms and ecstatic stream of consciousness. I could tell Pico was listening to her too as we lay in the darkness, at least three feet of empty space between us.

One night I heard another woman say to her,"You were my friend. Now you're just a 'ho."

In this box is the legal file on our building. A new owner took over last fall and began trying to drive us all out so he could co-op the building. Almost instantly it was war. Pico and I helped form a tenants' union. More than a hundred of us filed a petition with the city, protesting the rapid deterioration of services—lack of security, unsafe elevators, water and gas being turned off capriciously.

Pico took a strong interest in the disintegration of the building. It came on the eve of his own passage into the latter part of his thirties. There aren't many parts for aging Latin types. And he has a strong sense of family honor. This rent-controlled apartment is all his father had to pass on to the only son, and Pico takes every problem with it as a personal insult. Oddly enough, the trouble with the building seemed to loosen the tension between us. We were in this together.

In October the boiler was down and we had no hot water for weeks. In November we had no heat. We joined the other tenants for a candlelight demonstration in the hallways and invited News Center 4 to cover us. We hired a lawyer and began meeting with a judge. Pico had a spell of several months between jobs and was free during the day to represent the tenants' committee. He began to talk in legalese and bought his first serious suit. It was just about then that I got my big break.

There's a regular at the restaurant where I work who noticed that something about me had changed. He asked what was going on and I told him about my weight-training program.

"Sure has done a lot for your assertiveness," he said. After that he always dropped by my station to talk when business was slow. One day he told me about a casting call for muscular redheads. A two-woman show, on Broadway.

"Look, I'm not vain anymore," I said. "I'm thirty-three years old. It's too late for me now."

"You don't get it," he said. "This part is for someone who is middle-aged."

"I'm not that far along yet," I replied in a huff.

"You could pass," he said.

So I figured, why get hung up on a few years? And

I went. The director asked me to strip down to my bra and panties and hold poses.

"I'm not a body builder," I told him. "I just work out to stay in shape."

"Don't apologize. You're gorgeous," he said. "Can you run?"

"Sure."

"On a treadmill?"

"I do it all the time at the gym."

So I got the part. Half a dozen lines and I run for an hour and fifteen minutes while the other actress, who is famous, talks about herself.

The show opened in December and it was a hit. So there we were, the old fliparoo. I was at the theater six nights a week, sleeping until noon, working out in the afternoons. In the months since I'd been in the show, Pico hadn't scored.

"Look," I said one day. "We need two incomes." I meant it half jokingly. Pico scowled. The next day he said, "I do my part. Keeping track of the amount of rent to withhold for lack of services, that counts."

"Do more," I suggested.

He started cooking. Simple things at first, like eggs.

"Do you put the eggs in the frying pan before you turn on the gas or after?" he asked me one afternoon as I sat at the kitchen table drinking instant coffee.

"It's common sense," I said. "You fry eggs in butter. Butter melts with heat. Turn on the heat first and put the butter in. The eggs come later."

He didn't thank me, but he learned. From then on he offered me warm meals every day. And not long after he learned to cook, Pico had a break of his own. The tenants' committee had its first legal victory and he decided he had found a part he could play forever. He began to take night courses at the law school while I was at work. One day he told me he had a job as a short-order cook so he could cover his tuition. Not long after that he started coming at me hot and heavy again. I didn't turn him away.

So there you have it. You can buy a cruise guide for a buck, showing the major events of the marriage to date. We also have post cards for sale. Two versions. Pico slouching in the easy chair next to the Sal Mineo lamp, naked from the waist up, me standing behind him, stirring a pot on the stove. Or Pico at the stove, stirring, and you know who, strong and feisty, in the chair.

# ONCE IN A BLUE MOON

LIZA WAS SITTING on the steps of a townhouse on St. Denis Street in Montreal two doors down from a temporary outdoor bandstand, listening to Mack "Guitar" Andrews tease the crowd with a funky instrumental version of "Who Do You Love?" and musing about the enthusiasm with which the French Canadians greeted this second-, no, third-rate back-up band. They were the sort of musicians who usually played highway roadhouses and inner city taverns on Friday and Saturday nights while holding down nine-to-five jobs in city bureaucracies or working as short-order cooks in diners that opened at dawn. She was wondering how in hell they'd landed this gig without a vocalist. A guitar player had to be a genius like Clapton to hold an open-air audience for a two-hour set. And Andrews, a rotund ebony-colored man about five foot eight, with his sea-green polyester suit and maroon tie, didn't have the charisma or the licks to pull it off.

Still, the old yearning was in her when the drummer built up his backbeat and the young long-haired bass guitarist laid down the solid dark rhythm behind the leader of the band. The white kid on the bass was barefoot, wearing jeans and a Montreal Jazz Festival t-shirt. He was familiar to her, at least twenty years younger than the rest, one more youngster coming up on the road, burning his fingers trying to play the blues.

Washed by sound, Liza found herself focusing on the full moon rising over the St. Lawrence River.

Montreal reminded her of San Francisco. The sky seemed closer, the river's forking banks more evident than on the island of Manhattan, which continually diminished its natural setting. Living in New York, she hadn't seen a moonrise in months. With a sudden, novel sense of perspective, she contemplated the enormous warm yellow moon drawing to it the last rays of sun, pulling the tides back toward the land, water filling the salt flats and moistening the snarls of kelp heaped along the shores thousands of rocky miles away. This was the first of two full moons that July, an uncommon doubling event of nature—an extra chance for revelation or ruin, the way she figured it.

She felt mellow from the couscous and Moroccan wine they'd had at dinner. Stewart's theme for the night was French colonial. They were spending the week in Montreal so he could research a book on the French separatist movement. At dinner he had reminisced about the couscous he'd eaten on the Left Bank for a dollar fifty a plate, in the sixties. Stewart was one of the few Americans ever to complete a Ph.D. at the Sorbonne. "Lawrence Ferlinghetti and I," he liked to point out.

At the restaurant they sat on burgundy velvet cushions under an ornamental paisley tent.

"I used to wear clothes that looked like this room," she said.

"*Déjà vu*," Stewart said.

"*Déjà bleu*," she said. "Another glass of wine and I'll wax nostalgic about the original Fillmore and the free concerts in Golden Gate Park."

Sitting beside him now, she knew he was bored with Mack "Guitar" Andrews—Stewart preferred the cool abstractions of jazz—but she held him back when he suggested they head up the hill to their hotel.

"Not yet," she said. "They're not good, but I like the feeling here."

It was warm still, at least ninety degrees. The hottest day of the year to date. Montreal had waited ten long months to feel the heat of summer. This was the happiest solidly packed crowd she had seen since the first blissed-out days of 1967. Tonight they were in the grip of ecstacy, at the end of a sunny three-day weekend, drinking O'Keefe out of quart bottles and jiggling in the street unself-consciously. She was the Yankee cynic sitting among them eyeing the band with a practiced eye and finding it wanting. No, it did not draw her up and give her dancing feet. No, the drum did not enter her backbone and arrange its pattern along her nerve endings, Mack did not sear blank moments into her mind, like Jimi could—and where oh where was the thick-voiced singer to pull it all together, she was wondering, when Mack pulled out his ace in the hole, all the way from the Windy City, folks.

"And now, from the South Side of Chicago, an old friend of mine," Mack crooned into the microphone. The slight edge to his voice reminded her of the night at Basin Street West in San Francisco when she'd seen Dizzy Gillespie open for the Jefferson Airplane. "And now, ladies and gentlemen, I turn you over," Dizzy had said, making no attempt to disguise his contempt for the group of long-haired rockers who had bumped him from the headliner's spot. That edge said, I know what's going on here. Mack knew his band was a novelty act, a tiny raft of hip in a sea of pale northerners desperate for the low dip of sensuality. Mack could entertain the crowd, but he might have trouble checking into the city's better hotels.

A bushy-haired man of forty or so, barrel-chested, wearing blue jeans and a white cotton t-shirt, pushed past the drummer and the teenaged bass player, set a paper cup of beer down on an amp, took the microphone in his fist and began to sing.

The drummer perked up. The crowd grew quiet, sensing possibilities. A jolt of recognition pulled Liza out of her reverie. No one else in Montreal that night could know how far Mickey B. had come to sit in on the last set of the night.

"Sweet home, Chicago," he sang. "New York's got the people, DC's got the news, LA's got the stars but Chicago's got the blues. . . ."

Mickey B. was a chubby Jewish kid rebelling against a distant wealthy father when he began to learn the blues down on the South Side of Chicago in the early sixties. He'd hang around and jam, and they couldn't shake him, couldn't scare him away. He would carry cases and help set up and noodle on the piano and ask questions. Show me this, show me that. He never did learn how to read music; once he heard it he had it. He dropped out of his first year at Northwestern when they began to tour, breaking his mother's heart. He learned all about the pleasures of the boppers, the escape hatches to use when too many nights built into a solid crust of exhaustion—the inhalations, eventually the injections that could  calm him after a night at fever pitch.

When Liza met him she was a blank. Nineteen. Fresh from a small town near Sacramento. Might as well have been Nebraska, Iowa. Long pale hair, pale blue eyes, bare feet, floating down Haight Street, she was barely out of the cocoon of family, too unformed to have tried her wings. Drawn to her innocence, Mickey latched on, and moved her into his world of the night.

She liked to say, "I'm with the band." She helped them set up and get in and out of clubs. Eventually she handled the bookkeeping She was good with numbers. In the early dawn hours after performing the band retreated to Mickey's place, where they passed joints and drank Southern Comfort, Janis's drink, or peyote tea, and some of them snorted coke and a few disappeared into Mickey's bathroom and returned glassy-eyed and limp. None of them paid any attention to her. She liked hallucinogens, in mild doses, and they teased her when she showed up with velvety black dilated pupils stark against her fair skin. "Ah, Lady Liza is away for the weekend," they'd say.

Mickey's apartment in the Haight was a railroad flat empty except for a dozen high-backed chairs and an elaborate carved bed with a red velvet quilt. Mickey liked stroking her hair, her skin, rubbing her all over with this velvety fabric, nuzzling her like a horse.

The first summer they were together she followed Mickey and the band into the South. They played long nights in rough shacks surrounded by cotton fields, in white frame houses set  back from the road where the liquor was served in the kitchen along with cornbread and ham and the band set up in the living room. She kept track of the money and drifted along through the smoky nights. The local men in the juke joints eyed her, then backed off as if she were magically protected by Mickey and by B.G., who led the band.

They traveled at night and smuggled her in and out of cheap hotel and motel rooms like contraband. At the beginning of the trip concealment seemed like a game to her. She'd pile her hair under a newsboy cap and wear one of Mickey's jackets, just one of the boys. The first time she wandered out of the room she shared with Mickey onto the street to buy a newspaper B.G. pulled her back into the musty lobby and marched her back up the worn stairs to their room. "Look, girl, you're dynamite," he said. "You're here as a favor to Mickey, but I'll ship you home in a minute if you don't watch your step. You could get us all killed. Don't you go OUT without my say-so." He said "out" with the fury of a man who knew her presence could set a hellhound on his trail, and she finally understood the danger she posed, a young white girl with a mostly black band.

After that she stayed in the room reading magazines and napping during the days, while Mickey was busy with a tape recorder talking to the old-timers he found. He jawed with them about bottlenecks and slack strings and which eighty-year-old had influenced

Howlin' Wolf, about the regional variations in the music—Memphis, the Delta, Chicago, the Coast.

Once, in a hotel in Greenville, Mississippi, B.G. came to their room while Mickey was out. She was drying her hair when she heard the knock on the door. She opened up and let him in without thinking, assuming he would tell her what to tell Mickey when he returned, like she was invisible, just a message board. B.G. got a funny look in his eyes, reached out and circled her left nipple with his thumb, working as precisely through the thin fabric of her flowered shift as he did on his guitar strings, his eyes not leaving hers once. She froze. He dropped his hand and laughed.

"Careful, little girl," he said. "You might find yourself out of your element some day. Let Mickey know I want to see him."

During the years that Liza had drifted along on eddies of music, Stewart had been teaching at university sit-ins and hanging out at coffee houses talking about Mao and Marcuse. Listening to him sort out political declensions with his colleagues at City College now was like watching a skilled chef bone and fillet a trout. Her own political experience had been passionate but intellectually murky. She had put her body on the line repeatedly, in marches and demonstrations protesting the Vietnam war, the draft, racism, sexism. She didn't think twice about her resistance. As she grew older she realized she had been naive in some ways and careless in others, but she held onto a special fondness for her feelings until the early months of 1974. After that she thought of her life as growing up and getting over all of that.

Mickey had been busted for heroin that April, and although they had been together for more than three years, he didn't want her to visit him in Santa Rita, didn't want her to write. He sent B.G. to tell her he no longer wanted her in his life.

"Back off, little girl," B.G. said. "Man's got to get his thing together on his own. You need anything, you call me from now on." He smiled. His top two teeth were outlined with silver fillings. She didn't want him there when she cried, so she acted like she was fine and showed him out the door. She felt as if she'd been punched in the stomach. She stayed in bed for a few days playing the last brutal Robert Johnson album Mickey had given her over and over. It was simple in the end: I love my baby, my baby don't love me.

After a few weeks alone she covered her hurt with a thin crust of sarcasm and told her friends she had decided it was time to give up drifting and set out on her "real life." She enrolled at San Francisco State and found she could put her good head for numbers to use. When she finished there she went on to Stanford Business School on full scholarship. Swimming along in the wake of the first wave of women with MBAs she was offered jobs by half a dozen first-tier consulting firms after graduation. She took an offer to move to New York.

When she met Stewart, she was making a lot of money and living in a tidy one-bedroom apartment on

West End Avenue. She wore her hair in a cap of light curls and kept her papers in a leather portfolio. She liked knowing the ropes in business, and having her life sorted out.

Stewart was a surprise, arriving soon after she'd decided she should get used to being alone. They met at a screening of *Phantom India* at the Film Forum. She'd just returned from a hop-skip-and-jump business trip south. In Atlanta she'd counseled the head of a family-owned restaurant chain being circled by corporate sharks about the advantages of a leveraged buyout; in Charlottesville she'd met with a group of investors interested in starting a regional magazine. She'd spent so many hours in hotel conference rooms and on airplanes that her eyes were gritty and her skin dehydrated. On the way home from the airport in the taxi she'd started to weep from exhaustion. She decided it was time for a mental health day off.

She noticed Stewart on line for tickets in front of her—a wiry muscular man in black jeans and t-shirt, a tweed jacket, boots, with brown curly hair and a cocky attitude. She'd dressed down that afternoon—black jeans and a burgundy turtleneck, hardly any makeup. She had come to bury herself in the movie theater, so she hadn't paid much attention to Stewart, other than to make a quick urban scan telling her he didn't seem dangerous or crazy and registering his appealing profile. On line for coffee he was behind her. He spoke first.

"I saw this on television in France years ago. Have you seen it before?" he asked.

"Several times," she said.

"Here?"

"No, at the Surf in San Francisco."

"Oh, you're from Lala Land."

"That's Southern California."

"You blondes all look alike."

"Excuse me." She turned her back on him.

"Hey, I'm sorry," he said. "I've just spent four solid hours giving my introductory lecture to business majors on why study history, and I always get sour afterwards."

"You teach history."

"American history survey courses. Seminars in the liberation movements of the sixties in the U.S., France and Germany."

"Sounds archaic."

"You're telling me. It's depressing. And I was there. The students humor me when I lose my cool. It's unfashionable as hell to care about what you do, but I never got over the habit. Mind if I sit with you? I can fill you in if the subtitles are missing the point. I won't be obnoxious."

"Promise?"

"*Touché.*"

During their first weeks together he took her to a series of cheap Indian restaurants on East Sixth Street and sketched out his approach to the decades of the American century—the expansive forties, fueled by the war; the cool fifties. And then, he explained, with an economy overgrown like a lush jungle, with the seeds of another war and the expanded population of youngsters—the sheer mass of the first wave of the baby boom moving through the stages of adolescence—came the unprecedented conjunction of issues and mass behavior that was the sixties. He explained the chaotic period she remembered as the most magical and passionate time of her life as if it were an utterly predictable phenomenon of postwar America.

On their first morning in Montreal they ate breakfast at a French café down the street from their hotel instead of in the dining room, which served English-style eggs, bacon and grapefruit. Stewart wanted croissants and *cafe au lait*. He wanted to find eyewitnesses to the early days of the separatist movement. He wanted to speak French.

After breakfast they walked through Mont Royal Park, and saw a couple making love beneath a blanket, its edge hiked up to reveal a tangle of legs. It reminded Liza of Golden Gate Park, back then. Then Stewart took her to Parc St. Louis, across the street from their hotel, where the separatists had gathered for demonstrations in the sixties, and described the drama as if he could see it happening. On one side had been the party that wanted Quebec to be independent. Their leader was a former radio announcer named Rene Levesque who gave rousing speeches that rallied the working-class French Canadians. On the other side was Prime Minister Pierre Trudeau, who was French Canadian himself.

"Trudeau was a brilliant speaker in French and English," Stewart said. "He was a liberal, but tough in this situation. He said he would never allow the breakup of the state."

There were splinter groups on the left who used terrorist tactics—assassinations, bombings, kidnappings, death threats. "Trudeau cracked down on them, declared martial law in the province. There were arrests and trials. I remember reading about it in 1969 and thinking, This is Canada? I couldn't believe the violence, or the crackdown. To do it justice, I've got to understand how it happened."

The park was peaceful now. Clusters of gray-haired men in suits sat on the benches talking. Children played in the center. A film crew was shooting a cigarette commercial in one corner.

"How did it end?" Liza asked.

"There was a big referendum on whether or not the majority of the province wanted autonomy, a step toward independence. The pro-independence party suffered a humiliating loss, and the bottom fell out of the movement. Trudeau consolidated in no time. The most lasting result is that French became the official language of Quebec."

Liza shivered. As quiet as it seemed, this place was like those squares of land in San Francisco, Boston and Washington, D.C. where she had stood as part of a crowd, feeling the excitement of the voices raised from the podium, the tension of waiting for the tear gas and the clubs. Leading to what? The war ended, the draft ended, but beyond that it was difficult to pinpoint the changes. She could bring back the feeling in her own heart, but the rest of it, including the sense of being in this together that had characterized the times, had evaporated.

It would be up to a historian like Stewart, who had two sons he hadn't seen since they were babies and an ex-wife he referred to acidly as "that crazy Alice," to make sense of it all. Stewart believed there were lessons to be learned from history, that you could analyze human behavior long after the fact, reconstruct it even if you weren't there, figure out why they did what they did. Liza couldn't believe that, or much of anything else anymore.

As Mickey finished the last chorus of "Sweet Home Chicago," the crowd roared its approval. He paused to sip his beer, then shifted into a Willie Dixon tune, "Wang Dang Doodle." Liza was on her feet, swaying, trying to make him out in the darkness.

He was thicker through the middle, and his voice seemed raw even though he was only two numbers into the set. She wondered if he lived back in Chicago now, if he dropped by and sang with Mack for a few bucks every weekend. She wondered how many bands like this there were filling parks and lounges throughout the continent, how many musicians were still caught up in the drama of the blues, pounding out sounds so those who listened could soar above numbing routine—the mornings of coffee and newspapers, the brief or working lunch hours, the bosses who demanded too much and offered too little, the losses that came upon you so slowly you hardly even noticed.

Maybe Mickey worked for the post office and sang on Saturday nights. Maybe he was married with twin daughters, running his father's business now, and this was his vacation, maybe once a year he went back to the blues the way some people returned to favorite spots abroad.

For a brief instant she felt the old urge; she wanted to walk away from Stewart down to the front of the bandstand and catch Mickey's eye, she wanted to stay with him until he sang his last song and help him wind up the night with assorted uppers, downers, mind expanders; once more for old time's sake she wanted to lie in his bed wondering what they would do to each other and how it would feel. But even as she felt the impulse she countered it with reason. It made no sense.

Why did she feel sad to see that Mickey still was singing after all these years? She'd thought he might be dead. Out of the slammer, cleaned up or not, he was free, on stage and wailing away. Singing the blues.

The full moon had reached its midpoint, glittering cold white above them. It seemed much smaller now, distance weakening its pull. When Mickey finished, Mack put an arm around his shoulders, and Mickey bowed his bushy head in a familiar way, acknowledging the applause, then took another sip from the cup of beer on the amp.

A slim black man in a white linen suit, a man who seemed out of place in Montreal, stopped on his way past and gave Liza an appraising look. He looked like B.G. She turned her head, shutting him off as automatically as she shut her eyes at the end of each day, as completely as she had erased Mickey from her life all those years before.

Liza always thought of Mickey as having a small talent. But it was his. The incomparable Mickey D. No one else could sing the blues like he did, shading from lyrical foreplay into driving climax, throwing in quirky grunts at the end of looping lines. He'd worked at it, made it complete. His sound. She envied him that. She had never had anything like it. And he was doing it just for his own pleasure. In that brightly lit bubble of his music, the past receded and there was no sense of future, just the present, coming alive again in each performance. Tonight he was bringing her back with him to some place she had never been able to find on her own.

"Come on," Stewart said. "It's after midnight."

"Just a minute," she said. She was weeping quietly, holding onto the railing, jostled by people walking by, tears slipping down her cheeks into the darkness. She wanted something more before they went back to the hotel.

She wanted B. B. King in a helicopter descending onto the bandstand to play "The Thrill Is Gone" until the nerves along her backbone stretched full out into the darkening heavens; she wanted John Lee Hooker to materialize and sing in that rasping mean voice of his about a man's claim on his woman and the power she had over him; she wanted all the dead ones in a line back a hundred years or more—starting near to the present with Lightnin' Hopkins, just a few years in the grave—Howlin' Wolf, Memphis Slim, Robert

Johnson—one by one until dawn, with their variations on the basics, the true facts of life: he left me, she hurt me, we lost the joy we had now we get through each day somehow baby. She wanted to open it all back up and feel the hurt again.

# PAYBACK TIME

JONAH DIDN'T NEED an alarm to wake him at five-thirty, the buzz of anxiety in his stomach took care of that. He had no monster commute today, his flight to New York wasn't leaving until 11:30, but he couldn't sleep. What he wanted most now was time—late mornings in bed, Peet's coffee, sunshine on someone's hair. It was time to cash out. He was thirty. Every morning for the last six months he had wondered, Where did the last eight years go? Quarter by quarter, the valley had burned him out. Now it was just a matter of time until the big payoff.

He smelled coffee and padded to the kitchen, where his automatic machine had a double espresso all ready for him, punched in the night before for five thirty-five on the nose. The machine ground the beans, filled the little basket with the fine powder, forced boiling water at high pressure through the coffee until it steamed right into the little cup with his name on it, ready to drink just the way he liked it, extra strong. He headed into his office. The early June fog still hugged the streets outside. The headlights of a few early morning commuters sent out fuzzy arcs of brightness as they turned the corner onto Franklin Street. Poor suckers. He was glad he wasn't headed down 280 and back today. Instead of four hours in a car he'd spend five hours in a plane.

The computer fired up with a satisfying round of music and rolling digits, the final ping of the e-mail alert. He went to the web first to check the Hong Kong markets. Then he zipped into his portfolio. *The Wall Street Journal* said eMind stock was down ten points to 30 on rumors of a takeover. Time to snap up some more at a bargain rate. He went to redherring.com to see if there was any action on the eMind merger with 3f. It had been in the works for six weeks now. Nothing yet. Maybe that was good news. Once the deal went through, the stock could double.

He checked his e-mail. Several dozen urgent messages from the office, including one about the Funkyfish deadline. Something from his mother. Was it someone's birthday? Were his parents traveling again? They had just come back from St. Petersburg, where his father had attended a scientific conference. They had stayed with some down-at-the-heels former Soviet scientist to save on the hotel room even though the university was paying for it.

Jonah clicked open his mother's e-mail. Nothing new. Something about picking apricots. His parents had an old farm on the ridgeline a few miles up from Sand Hill Road, seven acres of apricot orchards and a stucco house with a red tile roof that needed work. They had bought it for a song in the early seventies, when his father, then a whiz-kid Ph.D. in physics at twenty-six, got the tenure-track job at Stanford. They talked fondly of the days when the valley was country.

His mother was inexplicably attached to the orchard. She always made a ritual of canning apricots each summer, pitting and peeling and boiling lots of cut-up fruit in big kettles on the stove, pouring the sticky mess into little jars, waxing the tops, putting on lids and handwritten labels. All she had to do was drive over to Draeger's and pick up anything apricot she wanted, from chutney to sorbet. But even though designer houses were nudging up to their fence, his folks were still in their time warp. Jonah nagged them to sell out and get something nice. They said they loved the space, they could never afford to buy so many acres, they didn't care if there was no central heating and the plumbing was old.

The phone next to his computer rang.

"This is Jonah." He checked the clock. Six a.m.

"Jonah? It's your dad."

"Right." He was being mighty formal. He usually called himself Toddy. Someone must be there with him.

"I'm in London, about to go to dinner. I hope I didn't wake you, I know you're an early riser, the commute and all."

"I'm up."

"Well, I know your mother won't be up yet, and I don't want to wake her. Would you give her a call later and let her know I'll be home tonight around six?"

"Right."

"How's everything?"

"Fine. Listen, I wanted to tell you about a deal I saw for you two."

"I'm on my way to dinner. Can it wait until I get home? How's the weather?"

"Rain."

"Damn! We've got that leak in the roof, she'll be beside herself."

"That's why I keep telling you to sell that place. It's falling apart, and it will just get worse. Listen, I found this horse farm near Woodside with several acres, they're asking a million four. But you've got to act fast."

"We can't afford Woodside."

"I've told you, if you subdivide you can make millions on the land alone."

"Pie in the sky. And what about our house? It's in no shape to sell."

"It's a disaster. A teardown. They'll build what they want anyway."

"Thanks but no thanks."

"Toddy. You don't get it." Jonah could never get through to him. "I know a guy who bought a house in Marin for $20 million cash, and it wasn't even for sale. He just wanted it and knocked on the door. You can get close to that for the land alone. Some venture capitalist could walk to the office from where you are."

No answer. The fucking pride of the man. He'd give him one more chance. "I could lend you the up-front money until you sell your place."

"I said no thanks. We've got what we want." His voice was steely. Jonah could imagine his jaw working.

"No regrets, huh Dad?" He didn't bother to keep the sarcasm from his voice. The connection ended. Bastard hung up on him. They couldn't care less. Toddy was a big pooh-bah in physics, but when it came to money, he was in the ether along with Tim Berners-Lee, the English dude who invented the World Wide Web but never saw the money in it. Toddy got exercised about access to the web, keeping it free. When it came to personal profit, making millions off what he knew, what he owned, he was clueless. And whenever Jonah talked to his mother about selling the house she brought up Chekhov, that Russian shit she loved so much. They could just stay put and act like the rest of the valley wasn't there. His friends had parents who set them up with their first good jobs, covered the down payment on a first house. He had to make his own way.

Silicon Valley was mostly orchards and the Internet was just a gleam in some bureaucrat's eye when Jonah was born. But he was in on the gold rush now. The valley had its own kind of biodiversity—semiconductors, software, biotech, the Internet. Semiconductors could be in the toilet, Internet companies on a roll. You just had to time it right.

Speaking of which. He had a few minutes to do a little work on the Funkyfish project. One of eMind's clients had a cool design with inch-high flashing fishes going across the screen, and he was trying to figure out how to put a blinking ad on the fish so it would seduce the masses into clicking onto his client's website and sticking there.

This was his second year with his third start-up. Reg, eMind's CEO, had talked him into walking away from the second just a few months before they went public, missing out on several hundred thousand dollars. Reg was a scrawny Georgia farm boy who went to Stanford on a scholarship in engineering and ended up at Hewlett-Packard. He retired at forty with a pile of cash and set up his own start-up, selling multi-million-dollar switches and routers to corporations for their intranets and hubs and networks. He went public the second year, and bought up all the little puppies until he was the biggest dog in the valley. Reg was sharp. He sat Jonah down over breakfast at Buck's in Woodside and ran the numbers through a spread sheet on his notebook computer, eMind versus the other company, and proved to Jonah it was worth it, even if his salary was shredded back to $80,000, because he'd be a VP and he'd end up with several million in stock options.

Jonah didn't think twice. Reg had a knack for impressing the Wall Street analysts and a reputation for winning big and rewarding his inner circle well. Now he wanted to nudge his hundreds of corporate clients onto the superhighway, teaching them to depend on the Internet for company-wide communication, for research, marketing, advertising, promotion, anything. He wanted to hit that jangling flashing jackpot again. Jonah decided to come along for the ride. eMind went public eighteen months in, and on paper Jonah was worth $3.5 million. He had to stay with the company two years to exercise his options. Only two months to go now. And there was more to come. He expected a bonus of five thousand shares when his promotion came through at the end of the quarter. After the merger, his options could double. And he had five thousand more shares coming when he hit his two-year anniversary. Then he could cash out and take his year off. This was the big score he'd been waiting for all these years. It made up for all the eighty-hour weeks, all the days without sunshine.

The anxiety was back once Jonah hit the airport a few hours later. The place was a construction mess. The shuttle buses from long-term parking were long and ugly, with surly drivers who didn't touch luggage. Next week when he flew to London to do the dog-and-pony show for the European clients he'd take the company limo to the airport instead of his Land Cruiser.

Calm down. He pulled a plastic pillbox and a bottle of water from the top of his briefcase, shook two capsules into his hand and swallowed with a swig of water. Good old kava. Some South Pacific tribe used it to get shitfaced. He used it to keep the little buzzes out of his stomach.

He wasn't scared. Scared was kid stuff. Anxious is what the big guys got. Even the mafia guys on *The Sopranos* got it. They didn't turn tail and run, they just took something for it and did whatever they had to do anyway.

Which reminded him. Time to fuck with Pete.

Pete was the other VP Reg had hired a few weeks back. Reg said the business was growing so fast he needed someone to take some of the load off Jonah. The first day Pete was in the office, Jonah invited him to lunch. Pete said no, he'd brought his own lunch. Macrobiotic shit. He spent his lunch hour reading. He had a stack of poetry books in his cube. Jonah noticed

Rimbaud, one of his mother's favorites. *Illuminations.*
*Une Saison en Enfer.* They were in the original French.
Pete wore Armani suits with ties and tortoise-shell
glasses to make him look like he had a brain.
Something not right about that.

Jonah was wearing an indigo blue polo shirt and
chinos for his trip to New York today to meet the CEO
of 3f, the French firm that was Reg's choice for the
merger. This was as dressed up as it got in the valley.
If 3f was going to do business with eMind, they needed
to know that.

Jonah pulled out his cell phone and hit speed dial
to the office. "I need a plane next Monday for an over-
seas flight," he said, as he scanned the signs outside the
bus. He was going to New York on United, was it?
"The company plane." Duh. Sally, his new assistant,
was such a dimwit. Being blonde and willowy wasn't
enough. He'd have to do something about her when he
got back from New York on Thursday. "I don't want to
go into Heathrow," he added. "Find an airport somewhere around there that will take a jet. Pete is going
into London for a Tuesday presentation. Get him onto
the Concorde."

That ought to fix weasel boy. Accounting always
frowned on the Concorde, might even veto his tickets.
Why didn't Pete use the company plane? they would
ask. Because I had it tied up—anywhere but Heathrow.
What Jonah really wanted to know was why Reg had
hired Pete. The only way to handle him was quick and
dirty.

"How's the merger deal going?" he asked Sally. No

news. He rolled his eyes in exasperation. "I'll check back in once I hit JFK."

He was meeting Felicia at the gate. Felicia was new. He didn't know why the 3f guys wanted to see her. She handled the company website, and an e-mail newsletter for 20,000 key clients. She was from the East, maybe Boston. An arty sort, thin, with long dark hair that tended to frizz on foggy days. Maybe he'd figure her out on the trip. Side by side for five hours, couldn't hurt. He wondered what she thought of Pete.

"They say yellow is the safest color for bikes," Felicia announced. They were buckled in, taxied and aloft, and Felicia finally relaxed her clenched fists.

"Why yellow?" he asked, humoring her.

"I guess it's easier to see. But white is the safest color for cars."

"White. My Land Cruiser is green."

"You don't drive one of those monsters!" Felicia's face grew pink with outrage. "Don't you know sport utility vehicles kill? Or don't you care?"

"Whatever." Maybe he wasn't going to figure out the mystery of Felicia. Maybe he could get some sleep. He pulled an eyemask and a bottle of melatonin from the side pocket of his computer case and waved for the attendant to bring him a new bottle of water.

"You're not going to take that!" Her face was aghast again.

"And why not?" He raised one eyebrow sarcastically.

"It's made from ground up cow's brains. You could get mad cow's disease."

"It's my brain." He snapped down his eyemask.

Dinner was being served when he woke up.

"So what's the hardest part of your job?" he asked Felicia.

"Keeping up on what's hot. You've got to know hundreds of sites, which ones are any good. You have to answer all the questions."

"How many hits do you get a day?"

"Fifteen, twenty thousand."

"Is that good?"

"Very good."

"What makes your website work?"

"It's easy to use. I think Reg is pleased."

She paused, gave him a significant look. She had a flicker of doubt? Reg was extremely easy to read. If he wasn't pleased, he went ballistic.

The attendant brought her a tray with lots of colors.

"What's that?"

"The vegetarian special." She unfolded her napkin carefully, set the tiny salt and pepper shakers to the right side of her tray.

He waited for her to ask, "And what's the hardest part of your job, Jonah?" He was the senior person here. And what would he say? Keeping all the billion-dollar clients happy by creating flashing Funkyfish to put their ads on, and interoffice memo forms in three languages. Making investors believe there was a there

there, when profits were a good two decades in the future. He was good at it. Because of him, the client base had grown ten times in the last year.

"You know Pete at the office?" she asked. "I don't like him."

"Why not?" he asked, trolling for allies.

"I had a long talk with him one day. The next day I was going for cappuccino and I ran into him and he didn't say a word. Same thing the next day. So finally I said, 'Are you avoiding me?'He didn't remember who I was. I've talked to him three or four times, he never remembers me."

So she was hot for weasel boy.

"He didn't know who I was for the first month, and I work in the office next to his," Jonah said. "He took over my clients when they put me in charge of Europe, but he acts like I don't know anything he needs to know."

"I think he's a womanizer type."

"He tries to come across that way, but he's not successful." Never pass up a chance to trash the competition.

"Really?"

"Really." What else? Herpes? Nah.

"I hear he's on the early track for Viagra."

"No." She seemed genuinely shocked.

"It happens. Eighty-hour weeks."

She was quiet for awhile, chewing her vegetarian cud.

He sliced into the chicken thigh on his plastic plate. It was covered with something red that smelled like fake smoke. He leaned forward over the tray table to keep it off his chinos.

"I've got an extra napkin," Felicia said, holding it out.

"I'm okay."

"I'm going to freeze my eggs," she announced.

"Is that some sort of vegetarian thing?"

"Eggs. You know." She raised her eyebrows. They were plucked in a fine line. "So they'll be fresh when I decide to have children. How about you?"

"Me?" What was she talking about?

"You know, your sperm."

"Freeze." Like diving into icewater. An involuntary shudder ran up his spine.

"You should think about it."

"It's a little early for that."

"How old are you anyway?"

"Thirty."

"Thirty is probably the peak." She smiled. "After thirty, you really should freeze it. You never know. By thirty-five real deterioration sets in."

"Let's talk about something else." Couldn't she see he was squirming?

"A headhunter called," she said. "A Boston job opening. She wanted me to FAX her a resume."

"And?" Jonah encouraged. She'd only been with the company three months. She didn't even know him.

"She told me I should get up there and interview right now, later this week after we wrap up. She said there were already two qualified candidates, she couldn't guarantee it would still be there. But I'm exhausted. I was in New York two weeks ago on my last trip, we ran and ran and ran, and now this one."

"What sort of job?"

"CFO for a start-up."

Jonah coughed.

"Are you okay?

"Piece of chicken went down the wrong way."

Felicia, the web manager, a CFO? She must be connected.

"Boston is very intellectual," she continued. "I went to school there. No makeup, women wear jeans and sweatshirts."

"Which school?"

"Two, actually. Wellesley. Then Harvard for my MBA."

Holy shit. She looked about twelve. Why was she in such a lowly spot? What was the point, about makeup?

"Didn't you work in New York?" he asked.

"Right. New York is like a movie, visually stimulating, everyone is all dressed up. But I got sick of it. I finally got a good apartment in a great building but the day I tried to move in the place was surrounded with barricades and secret service, the president was going to be coming by for a fundraiser. The guy in the penthouse had something to do with selling satellite components to China. Every time I entered the building I had to go through a metal detector."

"But the job in Boston?"

"I could do without it."

"So you like it on the West Coast."

"It's okay. I'm too tired to bother right now."

"Where do you live?" he asked.

Turned out she'd bought one of those cheesy live/work places on Potrero Hill. He owned a Victorian just off Union Street. He settled back, relaxed, as they bumped gently back to earth, enjoying the instinctive flexing of his body as the force of gravity caught up with them and they taxied into the gate.

The next morning Jonah was staring at someone's long dark hair on the pillow next to him. Who the hell is that? Then he remembered.

Felicia.

He'd offered her a lift to the hotel in the company limo. They were staying at the Plaza. He'd suggested an after-dinner drink. He had heard about this place that had twenty kinds of martinis. They'd just dropped in for a minute. The vegetarian chose chocolate. Who knew? She had two and reached for his belt right in the corner of the bar. He must have gotten her out of there fast. He had another shard of memory: her swirl of dark hair wrapped around his dick.

He didn't remember the rest. Too much time on the road? Jet lag? A bad mix of kava, melatonin and gin? All of the above? Now what would he do with her? She seemed to be deeply unconscious. Time to check the markets on his laptop. He threw on a terrycloth robe and went to the other room in the suite. There might even be time for a little trading before she woke up and he had to make conversation to get her out of there and back into her own room (she did have a room, didn't she?) before their nine o'clock meeting.

Jonah smiled; eMind stock was back up to $40. There was a knock on the door. He looked through the peephole. Room service. Good show. He must have placed an order on one of those menu cards they put on the pillow. Before or after? Whatever. The Filipino waiter rolled in a table shrouded in white and began whipping skillet-sized metal tops off the plates and fussing around with the coffee cups. Ah, time for the tip.

He went into the bedroom for some cash. The bed was empty. He could hear the shower running. Hey, this was his room, wasn't it? She could shower in her own. He dropped a couple of bucks on the waiter and showed him out, then knocked on the door. "Breakfast is served." He kept his voice pleasant.

She poked her head through the door wearing only a towel. She had the bathroom all steamed up. He hated that.

"I'll just have coffee, black," she said. "I'll drink it in here. Mind if I use your toothbrush?" She shut the door.

Now what?

"So you'll have to go to your room and change," he said firmly when he brought the coffee.

"No need. I'll just dry my hair and do my makeup and we can go."

"I'll need to shower, too."

"You look fine."

"Sure. How-de-do Mr. Collins in my Plaza Hotel robe."

He sat down to eat. Eggs and potatoes and melon and juice. He brought his coffee back to the desk and picked up the phone to check his voicemail.

"He's smart," he heard Felicia say to someone. "All these guys at eMind got 800s on their SATS and went to Stanford in engineering. He's got more on the ball than some of them. But he's jittery. I lay there last night watching his eyelashes twitch. Plus he's too thin, too freckled. Not my type."

"Not for you, sweetie," he heard the female voice on the other end say. "It's better not to get involved with any of them, it will only lead to trouble."

"Sometimes trouble is fun."

Jonah coughed. "I didn't know you were on the line," he said.

"I'll be just a minute," Felicia said, unfazed.

"Make it snappy," he said harshly.


The meeting at 3f headquarters was on the forty-fifth floor of a cantilevered building on 57th Street off Fifth. The floor-to-ceiling windows overlooked Central Park. No cubicles for these guys. He and Felicia sat on one side of the conference table, three guys in Armani suits on the other. She was in the black cotton pants suit she'd worn on the plane, he in his chinos and polo shirt. The air conditioning raised goose bumps on his bare arms.

Collins had pale skin, dark eyes with puffy grey circles underneath. As CEO of a Paris-based company, he spent most of his time in the air. He offered Diet

Cokes. Jonah said sure. Always go with what the head guy wants. Felicia asked for water. Collins ignored her.

"Too many chickens in the coop," Collins said. Funny, he didn't look rural. "We're going to have to make some hard choices."

Uh-oh, cutbacks. Jonah nodded. But he was telling them, so they must be okay. What did he want?

"I called you two in to cover some of the grey areas. Jonah, you were in on the ground floor at eMind, you know the soft spots, the expansion moves that didn't work. Felicia, you're in touch with all the current clients. Between the two of you, you're history."

Jonah winced.

Collins glanced at him and laughed. "Don't take that the wrong way."

Sure. You're history. Not my type. Two unexpected strikes in a matter of hours. Time to reassess the game-board.

Felicia was invited to step outside. Jonah started his boilerplate Internet speech. "The network is a network of networks, like a superhighway with off-ramps and side roads. It has twenty-nine commercial backbones interconnected at eleven official spots, and hundreds of unofficial . . ."

"We know," Collins interrupted. "We want to go over the numbers."

So Jonah and the three bean counters spent an hour going quarter by quarter through the brief history of eMind. They all kept a neutral tone. Just the facts.

Then Collins dismissed his sidekicks and asked the billion-dollar questions.

How did Jonah read the future of e-commerce? Of 250 milllion consumers, how many would buy on the net? "We're going for total saturation," Jonah said. "I just bought a Toyota Land Cruiser on-line, with extras—leather trim, power moonroof. This is only the beginning."

"How can you tell what's coming next?" Collins leaned forward. This was what was really on his mind, and he didn't want anyone else at 3f to hear the answer.

"Follow the military," Jonah said. "They don't worry about what things cost. If the military is trending toward band width expansion, or multi-user games in different locations, we'll all be going there in three or four years."

Collins sent Jonah on his way and called in Felicia.

Yes! Jonah felt like he'd aced an exam. He decided to take a walk before going back to the hotel. It was a hot day, nearly ninety, and humid compared to the West Coast, a definite novelty. A summer day in San Francisco was by definition cold and foggy. He strolled down Fifth Avenue, eyes glued to the store windows. He drifted into the Tiffany store and picked up a pair of canary diamond stud earrings for Felicia.

"Put it on my debit card," he told the salesman.

"Sir?"

"You heard me." He waved the card in front of his nose.

"That's an eighteen hundred dollar charge, we accept American Express, Sir, but not a debit card from an out-of-state bank." Cursing under his breath, Jonah pulled out his cell phone and hit speed dial for his banker.

"Charlie, tell this gentleman I'm good for eighteen hundred dollars." He handed his cell phone over the counter.

The clerk nodded, wrote down a series of numbers, handed the phone back.

"And did you wish that to be gift-wrapped, sir?"

"Damn right."

Felicia knocked on his door around six. "Do you have dinner plans?" she asked. "Let's try Babbo. Edward made us a reservation."

"Edward?"

"Collins. You know."

"Why not?" He was the one with the expense account, she knew how to pull the strings with Edward. Did she blow him, too?

"Give me half an hour to get presentable," she said.

"Wait. I have something for you."

"Mmmmm?" She stepped inside, close to him. He could smell the hotel shampoo, a slight tinge of sweat. She brushed her fingertips up the inner seam of his chinos and made a fist just below his balls.

"Whoa, wait." He went to the desk and pulled out the gift box.

"A present!" she called it out, excited as a kid at a birthday party. She sat on the couch in the suite and pulled off the gift wrapping, the ribbon, opened the special blue box.

"Ohhhh." At last he had her off guard.

She held the earrings to her ears. They brought out a yellow tone in her dark eyes, a fleck of some sort he hadn't noticed before. Was it wolves that had eyes like that?

"Jonah," she whispered. It was the first time she had used his name.

A few weeks later Reg threw a big bash for the eMind team. He rented the Exploratorium for the night, with a catered dinner, open bar, three bands, hot and cold hors d'oeuvres, large-screen videos all over of sharks and jellyfish and crashing surf. It cost almost half a million. A reward for all their hard hard hard work, Reg said in his speech.

Reg was a master at smoke and mirrors. But this summer he faced the worst of all conjunctions: At the end of the fiscal year July 1, with special scrutiny of the books now that they were public, it was painfully clear the sales staff hadn't made anywhere near their numbers. The analysts got wind of it, the NASDAQ got dicey for Internet companies and eMind stock went down to 8. A month after the bash, instead of eMind merging with 3f, Reg sold eMind to 3f outright. Edward Collins gave Reg an early retirement package of $30 million to sweeten the deal, and voilà, the French had a major position in the valley. The takeover news took eMind stock down to $4 a share.

For the first time in his life as he knew it, Jonah considered the possibility of prayer.

The Monday after that news hit, Pete knocked on Jonah's door and asked to see him. Jonah grabbed his latte and headed next door.

"So, Reg sold us out," he said, standing in the doorway.

"Sit down," Pete said. "It's payback time."

Jonah raised his eyebrows, sat down in the visitor's chair to the right of Pete's desk. Each cube had one. Pete had two.

"Jonah, I've been waiting a long time to tell you, you're outta here."

The buzz sparked in Jonah's stomach.

"Fat chance," Jonah said. "I went over everything with Collins; 3f needs me."

"Edward said to tell you, 'You're history.' His specific words. I can take it from here."

"Rat bastard."

"Sorry about the timing," Pete added, snickering. "Pity the stock tanked after our takeover." When he opened up his mouth and showed all his white white teeth Jonah thought of a shark swimmming toward him, thwarted only by glass.

So Pete was a spy from 3f.

"In fact," Pete continued, turning to gaze at his computer screen, "I think it's not through with the nosedive." He hit a few buttons. "Ah, here it is. eMind stock just opened at fifty cents." Jonah was speechless. His paper worth had vaporized overnight.

Even in his daze he was making quick calculations. Two months ago with the stock at 40 he'd been worth at least $4 million, now it was down to $40,000. Forget the five thousand shares for the promotion, forget the doubled stock options, he could go to court for the extra five thousand shares they owed him at the end of two years, since it was only a matter of weeks. But why bother, at fifty cents a share? Jonah winced. The buzz had repositioned itself as a sharp pain in his gut.

"No exit strategy?" Pete said, with a no-mercy smirk. "What's up with that? I thought you were the smart one."

Jonah stood up.

"What about Felicia? Is she out too?"

"Felicia? She was Edward's protegé, and this was her chance to shine. She scoped it out, she'll be in charge of the first French division we back."

The bitch. They were all in this together. No one at eMind saw it coming, not even Reg. Or did he?

In his office he found two security guys with blank faces removing his computer before he could download his files. Back home, he found two more on his doorstep waiting to strip him of his home computer and laptop and cell phone.

He felt like shit.

His net worth was down to zip, it could be months before the stock righted itself and he could negotiate for his options. Meanwhile he had the mortgage, the car payments, the rest. Time to go home to Los Altos and check in with good old Mom.


"Stanley Kubrick had fireworks at his funeral," Jonah's mother announced. "That's what I want." She was sitting on the patio in the shadow of a gnarly apricot tree serving iced tea and grilled chicken caesar salads to Jonah and her best friend Angela. His mother was slender and pale in her denim dress and sandals, her short dark hair smooth around her face. She looked more fortyish than fiftyish, except for the crinkly shit under her neck. He had hoped to find her alone.

"Cool," Angela said. She was small and vaguely red-headed, wearing a beige pantsuit. Angela taught twentieth-century American Lit. at Stanford. The two of them had been college roommates at Berkeley. They had been friends longer than he had been alive. He knew they could go on for hours.

"You probably need a permit," his mother continued. "Unless it's around the Fourth of July. I wonder what it takes."

"Fame. Maybe it's easier in England. We were in Cambridge in the summer and they had fireworks, just to celebrate some anniversary."

"If not fireworks, something. Sparklers. Hand them out to everyone to light up at the end."

"I can see it. Better if it's at night."

They were laughing now.

"Unbelievable," Jonah muttered into his Romaine. He couldn't imagine his mother dead, and here she was laughing about it. The buzz in his stomach worsened. It was constant now. He was off caffeine even, trying to keep it down.

"Oh, don't mind us," his mother said, bent over with hilarity. "Is a night funeral more formal?" she choked out. "I don't want people dressing up on my account."

"We could light them at the cemetery?" Angela had taken a small notebook from her tote and was taking notes with a yellow pencil. She probably didn't even know how to use a Palm Pilot.

"I guess so. After I'm planted. I haven't made that decision, actually. Fireworks is easy. That's the only definite."

"Cremation or burial? That is the question," Angela said.

Jonah pushed the nine-grain croutons to the side of his plate and tried to think about something other than his mother's funeral. How could she talk this way in front of him? She had expected Angela for lunch, but not him, so he was stuck. He couldn't leave the table until coffee was served. House rules. And he needed to explain what had happened at eMind. He needed to borrow some money until his stock went back up. He knew they must have something stashed away. They'd paid the house off, they bought their ten-year-old Peuguot outright, they never spent money. She was an easier touch than his father. His father hated talking about money. He thought Jonah had taken the dirty path. It really burned Jonah. They had the wrong house, the wrong car, the wrong everything, all because his dad had never made a dime.

"Both," his mother said. "Maybe. Actually cremation is cheaper. That could make a difference. But I don't want to be scattered about."

"So you need a plot of ground somewhere."

"Here in Los Altos."

"Have you bought it?"

"Not yet. I wonder if there are any left. I may have no choice but be scattered. If so, I'd like it to be here in the orchard." She gestured toward the trees that grew all the way from the house to the road. Jonah had always wished for a front yard instead of all those trees.

"I hope you're paying attention," Angela said tartly to Jonah.

"Right. Like I want to think about it."

"Now, Jonah," his mother soothed. "You'll think about these things too . . ."

"When I'm your age. I know."

On some level he could tell they were being serious. Telling each other something in that way women do. It was something he could never be part of and that pissed him off. Especially now, listening to them talk softly, comfortably, about dying.

"I suppose I'll outlive Toddy," his mother said. "I don't understand why my mother is still alive and my dad is gone. They were the same age, ate the same things, drank the same water. He did diets, exercise, she sat like a lump, couldn't keep her mouth shut around sweets, and outlived him by ten years so far."

"Male genes, heredity, all that," Angela said.

"Hey, watch it!" he said. When would this end?

"Sorry hon. It's part of the basic unfairness of life etcetera." There she went again, with her infuriating way of referring to big subjects in trivial terms, tossing them off with a little "and so forth" but not explaining. It was a shorthand he never had learned. He gazed at the tree by the side of the patio. A few shriveled reddish apricots clung to the thorny branches. The trees didn't even bear fruit like they used to.

"Langston Hughes died of uremia," Angela said. She was writing a critical reassessment of Hughes. "He went into the hospital under a pseudonym with a prostate infection and something wrong with his heart, and by the time someone recognized him he was dying. Uremia."

"So he didn't have to die."

"But he did."

The two of them nodded and were quiet for awhile.

"He was ready," Angela added. "He wrote his will out four years before. I just got around to mine yesterday. I did one of those cut-out-of-the-workbook dealies a few years back before taking off for London, just so there would be no confusion, left it on the dining room table. When I got home, I stuck it under a stack of papers."

"Why is it so important that everything is 'in order?' If you're gone, what's your worry?" his mother mused.

"What about me?" he asked.

"Oh, for the survivors, yes," his mother reached over and patted his hand. The buzz was increasing now.

"It focuses anxiety on lists and estate taxes, not death, I suppose," she added to Angela.

"Any movement on selling the house?" Jonah asked.

She looked at him blankly.

"I talked to Dad about it," Jonah continued. "You really ought to talk him into selling. I could do it for you."

"Do what, hon?"

"I could get a realtor's license and find a buyer. It

would be too easy." And the ten percent fee would carry him through for months.

"Seriously Jonah, I don't know what's got into you. We like it where we are."

"You could make millions, retire, anything you want."

"We have what we want, hon."

"I'll talk to Toddy about this."

"You won't get anywhere. You know that."

She was right. The two of them frustrated him beyond belief. "When are you going to wise up?" he said, not bothering to disguise the edge in his voice.

She fixed him with her cold look, one eyebrow raised. "This is our home. You don't have to like it."

"I think it's just blankness," Angela said. "Nothing."

"What?" Jonah was dizzy. His palms were wet. He had a horrifying thought. They would never change.

"You know, death," Angela said.

"I think it's something we can't imagine," his mother said, sliding back into neutral. "What I hope is it's like that euphoria you get when you're having a great dream, and you get to stay in it."

"Doubtful," Angela said with a cynical laugh. "So much is fucked up here, how could it be any better afterward?"

"I think words like 'better' don't mean anything after you're dead," his mother said. "It's more like 'infinity.'"

"We sound like sophomores," Angela said. They were laughing again. How could they?

"I feel like a sophomore," his mother said. "Why do I have to change how I feel just because I'm older?"

"A lot older. Try thirty years."

"Okay, a lot older. There are all these rules. You have to retire at what is it now, seventy? Sixty-eight?"

"Who can afford to retire? I just hope I can keep mobile enough to work until I drop dead."

"You can't drop dead—that was a nineteenth-century luxury. It's not allowed now. They'll plug you into machines."

He felt a surge of rage toward his mother. She would never understand what he was going through. She had never worked like he had, twenty-four/seven for years, and then had someone hit delete. She had lived this easy life, with Toddy and the apricot orchards, and some day she might be hooked up to a machine, her body a wreck, her eyes pleading, and he would have to figure out what to do.

The buzz was a pain now, steady and true. It was not going to go away.

"'What about me?" Jonah said, louder than he'd expected. "Here I am dead meat and all you can talk about is fireworks and cremation."

The two woman swiveled shocked faces with round eyes and mouths toward him in tandem, like they were attached to the same invisible string and somebody had yanked the cord.

"Jonah, honey," his mother said, reaching her hand out with a soothing gesture.

He pulled away and stumbled to his feet."When are you going to wake up?" he yelled as he headed around the side of the house to his Land Cruiser. Didn't they get it? The clock was ticking.

It was only a matter of time before it all fell apart.

# MEMORIAL DAY

THAT SUMMER PROMISED to bring the worst drought of the century, worse than the dust bowl. The leaves dried up and fell from the trees. It was like something biblical—a plague of locusts, famine, drought. Animals roamed far beyond their normal boundaries. Mosquitos brought tropical diseases to the city. The earth's crust hardened. Then came rains. Floods. Unnatural disasters.

That summer, for the fourth time in as many years, their son was in trouble. He was twenty-eight and lived thousands of miles away in Oregon, but his problems burrowed into their deepest selves, forcing them to question everything they knew. This time two people were dead.

"I have the terrible feeling that something is about to be over," Maureen said. She had been silent through most of the long hot drive from the city to the mountains on that sunny Memorial Day. How did she know? Something about the line of the horizon, the clouds over the distant mountains.

"You'll feel better after you get some rest," Jeffrey said.

"I wish I could hibernate until it all goes away," she said.

They arrived at their destination, a slightly bedraggled village kept alive by a ski resort, in the late afternoon, cranky from traffic and the first scorching heat of summer. They got out of the car, stretching.

They were a handsome couple in their late forties. She was fair-haired, her attractiveness subdued in some way, as if a light had been dimmed. He was olive skinned and fit, light haired enough that they once had been taken for brother and sister. The realtor's office was closed, but just as she had promised, she had left an envelope under the mat. Jeffrey opened it and pulled out the lease and two keys. He raised his eyebrows and pointed to the line that included the address of the ski chalet.

"Rob this place," he said. "I'm glad we got to the key first."

"It's a small town," Maureen said.

They had rented the place sight unseen for the month, desperate to get away. It was easy to find, halfway up the winding slope, a three-story chalet with green trim.

Inside, it was blessedly cool. The place was airy and light, with decks on each of the three floors, a living room and dining room  with a cathedral ceiling and wall-to-wall carpeting in a pale color that might be considered oyster. Green couches on a red patterned area rug. A round oak dining table with six matching chairs. A fieldstone fireplace that would be the warm center of the house in winter.

Then she noticed the two massive pine wreaths on the fireplace, the mantelpiece lined with red and silver ornaments, big bowls of candy canes, Santas and elves here and there.

"I suppose this is what we get for renting a ski place in summer," Jeffrey said wryly.

"They must use the house in winter," she said. What seemed normal in December looked out of whack. "You'd think they would take them down before they leave." The holiday decor continued throughout the house: pillows with "Let It Snow" in needlepoint on the couches, four-foot porcelain reindeer with bells and ribbons at the foot of the stairs, red and green dishes, wallpaper with stars and snowflakes, a painting of Father Christmas over the king-size bed in the master bedroom.

It was a house just for Christmas, inhabited by a large family, she learned as she followed their lives from room to room, glancing at photographs on the walls and tables. In the earliest snapshots, the four children were toddlers, the parents round-faced young adults; then came graduations, weddings, grandparenthood. One of the daughters turned out to be the spitting image of her mother. Each year there were photos of them all in ski outfits, with beaming faces. They came back here to drink hot chocolate in the morning and martinis at night and sit around the fire.

There was even a Christmas tree on the deck.

"I don't know if I can take this," she said. Tears came close to the surface. Jeffrey opened the sliding glass door to the deck and went out to take the tree down, but it was held firmly in place with guy wires. It was a rusty brown, its needles soft and weathered. There were two bird's nests high up in its branches.

"I'll take it down in the morning and store it away somewhere," he said.

There was a television in the corner by the fireplace, its relentless red power light blinking. She unplugged it and turned on the radio. The last passages of Benjamin Britten's "War Memorial" filled the room, the boy sopranos and mournful contraltos remembering the dead, the final chimes.

And what about the living who are lost to us?

The trouble was bad enough when Peter had called to tell them he was in jail. It got worse when he called to ask for her help in the trial.

"It's up to you now," he said. "If you don't save me, I'll know you're on their side."

"But I don't know anything about what happened."

"You could be there for me," he said in his charming tone. "Weren't we together? You were visiting, or I was on a trip back to see you, you could say I wasn't even in the state."

"I can't do that. And wasn't it your car?"

"You're going to hang me out to dry?"

"It's not about me."

"It's all about you, Mom," he screamed so loud she had to hold the phone away from her ear. "You're lying now," he continued. "You've always had secrets, and when I need clues the most, you won't lift a finger to help."

"What secrets are you talking about?" Was he drunk? Was he so stressed out that the medication wasn't working? Had he stopped taking it again?

She felt the sick helplessness return. He was back in a whirlwind of chaotic thinking, throwing out anything he could think of to hurt her. In some eerie way it was as if he were forcing her to feel how he felt.

"Family secrets. You know, and you're not telling." It was one of his obsessions.

"What are you talking about? I told you everything, probably more than I should have."

She reminded him that she had told him about the divorce at several ages, beginning when he was four, a few years after she and Evan had split, again when he was seven and she and Jeffrey were married, again when he first got into trouble as a teenager. She had told him about the time she had tried LSD in college and decided not to do it again, the fact that everyone in college smoked a little pot.

"Words words words words words! Tell me the truth, you bitch!"

She bent over as if he'd punched her. He had never called her names, never crossed that line.

"Time out," she said. "Time out."

"What does that mean?" he shouted. Again she had to hold the phone away from her ear. "Does that mean you're taking off like you always do? "

"It means I don't want to speak with you for awhile."

It was better than hanging up on him. It was self-protection.

"You had to, for your self-esteem," her friend Barbara had said later. Barbara had raised three kids on her own."You can't allow him to talk to you that way."

"But he's sick, he's in trouble, he's frightened."

"Even so."

"I'm his mother."

"Even so."

"It's unbearable."

"Even so, it will pass."

"I can't believe that. I feel as if I've lost him forever."

She didn't expect to speak to him anytime soon. This could be a long time of estrangement, depending on what she decided to do. But that didn't mean she didn't think about him and puzzle over what had happened.

She remembered him at twelve, thin and rangy as a colt, suspicious of the next door neighbor who wanted to play baseball with him. Within a few years he'd grown to over six feet tall and he wasn't just quirky, he was ill in some insidious way. He was filled with rage over little things. One night she came into the living room when he was watching a football game and changed the channel to check the weather forecast. He freaked out. He stood over her, shaking and screaming, and when she tried to get up from the couch he grabbed her shoulders and shoved her back down so hard she bounced. She sat dazed and terrified, looking up at his jaws opening and closing, his face scarlet from anger, and she knew that he could be dangerous.

The therapist she found told her that her son saw the world in black-and-white terms and would, from time to time, fall into delusions, the content of which would vary, with friends and foes delineated in different ways. The condition would ebb and flow, but it was treatable, with medication, if he took it.

"Is he crazy?" she asked.

"This is just how your son is wired. It's like his radar is jammed, he confuses friends with foes," the doctor said.

She tried to make sure he took the pills each morning until he moved away. How could she know if he was taking them now? He lived on another coast.

"And what about the drinking?"she had asked the therapist. Peter had started going out after school with some kids from his class and and coming home drunk.

"Self-medication."

The therapist was clear, precise. He didn't have to live with the mess.

She was glad her parents weren't alive. What would they have made of a son who was always "in trouble?" Her mother would have been ashamed. Her father might have tried to understand. The two of them had been old at thirty, raising four children on a parson's wage; she had vowed it wouldn't happen to her, that she would break through the rules that had tamped her parents down.

His therapist used to tell her not to take her son's attacks personally.

How could she not, when he was calling her a liar? When he was making up this idea of her keeping secrets when she hadn't?

When the rages passed, he didn't remember. She did.


In the late afternoon, as she lay on the living room floor to do her back exercises, she heard the wind rustling in the birches. Not the sound of traffic, or cell phones, but natural sounds. She heard birds, and water in the runoff creek. The quiet was a relief.

Jeffrey had coached her: "Say, 'Peter, I love you, but you can't talk to me that way.' Draw the line. You must do that for your own self-respect. Tell him, 'You can't inflict that kind of pain and expect me to take it.'"

"You're right," she said. "I wouldn't take it from anybody else, not from you, or my boss. I don't know what happens. I freeze. I can't cut him off. I'm worried about him."

"You have to do it."

She thought of Jeffrey, reassuring Peter when he was sixteen: "Any time, day or night, just give me a call and I'll come get you. I don't ever want you to feel like you're trapped." Peter had been drinking beer in a local bar when a fight broke out and somebody was stabbed. The cops picked him up with several other under-age kids and called them to pick him up at the station. The three of them sat at the kitchen table drinking coffee until dawn. Peter was quiet, his face ruddy with drink, his eyes drooping. Jeffrey, who had grown up in a tough mining town in Pennsylvania, was firm. "You're over your head and you don't even know it," he said. "There are certain things that you can do that I can't help you out of. There's this invisible line, and once you cross it, there is no way out. Don't get in that situation. You're in a bar and someone has a gun? Get out of there. Somebody thinks you're after their woman, he pulls a knife? Leave. Lie if you have to. You don't have to be the big man."

Maureen was grateful Jeffrey took charge. What did she know of knives, of bars? Jeffrey's approach seemed to work when Peter was younger. Now it was too late. He had crossed that invisible line.

Earlier in the year, when he had called to rail against his boss, a smart skinny blonde, she had sensed he'd lost his balance. He said the boss had called him in and said she would have to let him go if he didn't take his medication at least twice a week.

"No way," he had said. "The bitch."

"Why did she do that?" she had asked. Why did the boss know about his medication? How bad was he? "Did something happen? Why aren't you taking your pills?"

She had not been able to make sense of his answer, something about not getting what he had coming in the way of his bonus.

The accident had come a few months later.


She remembered him as an adolescent fighting the air around him with frustration. Now he was a violent man. Was it her fault?

The bad seed, that was what they used to call it. Now it was a gene gone awry. Too many Xs or Ys, or a squiggly where it didn't belong. Sin, the devil, evil, were old-fashioned terms. This was the brave new world of electron microscopes that could look inward with as much power as we looked outward into space. Now it was black holes of the psyche, caused by DNA, something invisible to the naked eye but destructive as a cyclone.

Was it possible that her boy had never had a chance, that he was just born this way?

The sky was apricot at sunset, bathing the birch trees across the slope in warm light. She could see some fallen trees, bent into strange shapes. Last winter's winds had been fierce up here. She sat on the deck watching the shadows of clouds play across the distant peaks. In the nineteenth century, painters had been drawn to these gentle green mountains misted by low-lying clouds, and despite the intervening grind and clatter of civilization, the range had remained undeveloped except for the ruts of ski slopes and the clusters of chalets. She could see the village, with its tiny steeple and red barn and white frame houses.

Jeffrey brought her a sandwich and a glass of iced tea. Eventually the rim of mountains turned dark and it was time for bed.

She couldn't sleep without something—valerian, melatonin, antihistamines. She would take only herbs or over-the-counter things, nothing as strong as prescription sleeping pills. She was supposed to call Peter's lawyer in a week. He said the trial date would be set by then. Between now and the start of the trial she had to decide what to do.

"You have to let him bottom out," Jeffrey said as they lay in bed that night. "Take the consequences."

"If it means going to jail? He couldn't handle that."

"You mean you would give him an alibi? Lie for him?"

"I don't know."

"That's the coward's way out. It won't help him."

"It could keep him out of jail. His lawyer said he could get up to fifteen years for hit and run, drunk driving, maybe manslaughter."

"And you could end up charged with perjury."

_____

She woke to delicious cool air. The room felt spacious and empty except for Jeffrey at her side. She listened to his breathing. His chest was leaner than when she first had known him, but still muscular. His legs were well muscled, too. Without too much effort he had hardly any body fat, while she spent hours at the gym.

She felt calmer at last. The worry about Peter had abated. The steady stream of routine but urgent detail that filled her days as head of the political science department at the university had dried up for a brief moment.

Later that morning Jeffrey set out to remove the Christmas tree from the deck. She was in the upstairs bedroom drinking coffee when she heard him cursing. She rushed downstairs and found him staring over the edge of the deck.

"What happened?" she asked.

"The babies." He pointed to the grass under the deck, smashed remains, a pink and red mess with bits of shell and fluff. He sat on the bench and buried his face in his hands. His shoulders were shaking and he made sounds she'd never heard before.

That night she drank two glasses of wine with dinner instead of her usual limit of one. Afterward, getting frozen yogurt from the freezer for dessert, she noticed three bottles of vodka chilling. Vodka was her father's drink. She never touched it. She drank bourbon a little in her teens, she drank beer in college, but it was fattening. Red wine gave her headaches. Sometimes she drank white wine or a spritzer.

She wondered what it felt like to get drunk and drive and wake up the next morning in jail and know something terrible had happened. To not remember anything but to have to face it.

She poured herself a glass of orange juice, added ice and an inch of viscous liquid from the icy bottle. The juice would mask the taste, wasn't that the point? Three times she did it, wondering, Is this what he was after? She felt dizzy and miserable.

Enough.

She was weeping in an easy way, unabashed, pure.

"What is it?" Jeffrey asked.

"How could this happen? Remember how sweet he was?"

"Hush," he said, stroking her back. "It's not your fault."

Jeffrey had grown up in a family of drunks—his mother, father, two brothers and a sister. He had dodged the bullet. He didn't drink at all. But he felt responsible for all of them years after he left home. They called at all hours, his sister in an emergency room with slashed wrists after a binge, a brother locked up for fighting again, could he send money? Maybe that's why it wasn't so hard for him to take on another man's son as his own. Jeffrey had raised Peter. Jeffrey was his father. But he wasn't responsible in that scientific way, for the genes.

———————

The sound of birds woke her. One had the sound of a whistling teakettle, another a monotonous chirp chirp chirp. The eastern sky was stained with pink. Her head ached. But nothing terrible had happened.

A shaft of sunlight spilled over the rounded mountains at just the right angle to find its way through the vertical fabric blinds to shine straight into her eyes. She flinched. It was like someone had taken aim and thrown a dagger.

"We could just stay up here, be lost, where they can't find us," she whispered. "We could stay up here until the trial is over."

"Shhh. Go back to sleep."

"I can't."

She took an aspirin, and lay there trying to make her mind go blank. She could wait and hope that maybe, against all odds, this would all go away, her son would come back to himself and get out of this mess, that some day  he would forgive her the sins he had imagined.


When she woke again Jeffrey was already out of bed. She flipped on the radio. Haydn. It was seven-thirty and seventy degrees already. The day would be muggy, in the nineties. She heard the car start. Jeffrey was on his way into town for the newspapers and coffee. She was afraid she might drive him away.

Looking for shorts in her bag she found the manila envelope of Peter's letters. Crazy outpourings, addressed to her. They had been coming daily for the past month. One more reason she had to get away. She kept them with her, as evidence? Just in case?

Was he dangerous? she had asked his therapist when Peter was living with them. Was she safe? Was Jeffrey safe?

"As long as he's taking his medication."

"How can you be so sure?"

"The medication keeps symptoms under control in ninety-eight percent of the cases."

"Under control," she had learned, was a relative term, known only to those who lived with him. Just in case, she had made sure there was no way for him to find out where they were now. She figured they would be safe here while she sorted things out.

She thought of Evan. Peter had his father's nervous energy, his probing mind, twisted in some way. Evan had seemed dangerous at times. She remembered being twenty-two and terrified, feeling she was taking her life in her hands by leaving him. Peter was just a toddler. Excited by his first Christmas tree, he had grabbed a red glass ornament and knocked the tree over. Evan exploded. She grabbed Peter and shielded him from his father. "He's just a baby,"she shouted.

She left a few weeks later. She planned it carefully, packed what she would need, and one morning she just drove off down the freeway and took a snow-clogged county road to the end and found a hiding out, deserted place on a frozen lake on the outskirts of a village so far from civilization he'd never think to look there. She hid out for months. It was the only way she could think of to decide what to do. When spring came, she filed for divorce.

Now she had run away again. For how long?

She had lost track of time. She decided to walk early, before the heat grew unbearable. The rhododendron bush in front of the house was beginning to show hot pink buds. The lilacs were blooming along the path she took to the top of the mountain. The air was still and hot. She saw a large bird ahead of her on the path, head bobbing forward and back, then another. She counted twelve wild turkeys, two parents and ten babies. They straggled in a line across the path and into the woods. Toward the top of the slope she spotted the scat of some animal along the path. It was black, like a long scrape of tar.

Going downhill was a breeze, once she found the rhythm. As she headed up the steps of the house she noticed the garbage can had been knocked over. She picked up the bottles and paper napkins and put them back in, locked down the lid. Peter had told her about raccoons coming for food in the night at his place in Oregon.

She wished she could have slowed time down when he was a child, observed better, recognized what was coming, stopped it somehow. Round and round she went. She and Jeffrey talked it through over and over, then one of them would say, "Enough, we have to stop thinking about him." They would drift into separate corners, still thinking about him.

Jeffrey was patient until the first time Peter called them from a jail cell in the middle of the night. It was his freshman year at college in Eugene. Jeffrey said,

"We all make mistakes, but this had better be the last time." There was a lull. Then another call. Drunk driving. She wanted to fly out, help him find the lawyer. Jeffrey refused. The two of them fought bitterly. "If he's old enough to get into this kind of trouble, he's old enough to find his way out of it," Jeffrey said. She could see the point, but it hurt.

The third time, Jeffrey refused to take the collect call at 3 a.m. and held the phone away from her. When she wanted to call the jail the next morning, Jeffrey convinced her to wait. Peter called a week later to say he was going into a program. Court orders. They decided to try a support group, to help him, but they learned that was not what it was about at all. It was about detaching from him, turning him over to the Higher Power and going on with their own lives. Most of the other people in the group were adult children of alcoholics, not parents of adult alcoholics. It didn't make sense. Before they stopped going they learned some useful phrases. Don't dial up pain. Poor me, poor me, pour me a drink.


She was jolted awake by squealing and roaring, loud thumping. Someone was being killed.

Jeffrey was at the sliding door to the deck in his shorts, peering out.

"Who's out there?" she whispered.

She got up and stood next to him, still muddled with sleep. He shined a flashlight outside. She saw a creature about Jeffrey's size, with fur. She smelled a wild animal stench, some combination of mold and rotten, decaying meat.

"It's a bear," Jeffrey breathed into her ear. "Not a grizzly. A black bear. He's after something up that tree, probably a squirrel or a raccoon."

The sound was horrifying. She started to slide the door open.

"Don't let him see you move," Jeffrey hissed. "He might think you're something to eat. They can climb. He could come after us."

The bear raged, the tree shook, the creature was caught and she heard the bloody crunching of jaws.

Jeffrey's solid body next to hers in the darkness made her feel safe, but was she really?

"What should we do?" she whispered. It wasn't like the city, where you simply called 911. Jeffrey was from a place where people knew about wild animals. She was a city girl. She had never imagined nature bloody in tooth and claw under her bedroom window.

"There's something wrong with him," Jeffrey said. "He might be rabid."

"Or crazy," she said.

The darkness grew quiet. They went back to bed, lying gingerly on the white sheets. She drifted off and woke again to more roaring and squealing. It was 2:11 on the bedside clock. For the next hour they stood huddled together at the door watching the bear chase, catch and devour another raccoon. His sheer animal force was unbelievable.

"I can't take this anymore," she whispered at last.

"We could make noise. That's supposed to drive them off."

They went downstairs to the kitchen cupboard, pulled out pots and pans and  went back upstairs to start a clatter. She pounded away at a lobster pot with a wooden spoon, Jeffrey banged two lids together. She stared into the blackness. Nothing. Was he gone?

The third attack came around four. He roared, he charged, the raccoon screamed in terror. Maureen's heart beat so hard she thought she might die. She was exhausted. She just wanted them to get through the night alive.

As the light came at dawn he seemed to evaporate.

"Do you want to come into town for breakfast?" Jeffrey asked.

"I have to get some sleep." He stayed with her until she drifted off.


When she woke again Jeffrey was back with gossip from town.

"Drought brought the bears down low," he said. "I knew there must be something wrong. A family of three have lived in a den on the other side of the mountain for years. They never gave anyone a problem. But the water dried up, and they started roaming."

"You're telling me it was just the drought that made him show up here and act like that? That's hard to believe."

"In some places they've been known to come right into town and cause trouble at garbage dumps," Jeffrey said. "When they get used to eating human food, they're really dangerous. He knew we were here. They can smell us from miles away. Usually they don't want anything to do with humans. There might be something else wrong with him."

"I don't care," she said, suddenly furious. "He was murderous. It doesn't make any difference why."

"He was probably starving," Jeffrey said.

"I said, I don't care. If we had been in his way, he would have killed us, too."

Jeffrey looked at her, perplexed, and she realized how angry she sounded.

"Two people are dead," she said savagely. "A young woman and her baby." She had to stop for breath. "Because of him. And I'm his mother."

The day before she wasn't sure, but now she felt a click deep inside. The roulette wheel of choices slowed and the ball fell into place.

She would let Peter's life follow its course. She would do nothing to fix it, nothing to push it forward. He might go to jail for up to fifteen years. He would have to face the victim of his actions—the woman's husband, the child's father. She could not protect him from any of it. He would not believe this. Later, she could write him in jail, send him books, and never hear from him. Her choice could make her the enemy forever, which would sadden her beyond imagining, but for now she knew there was only one thing to do.

Nothing.

# WINTERING AT MONTAUK

MONTAUK WAS THE solution. He had no job, no money. He could stay for the winter at the summer place. It would be a lark.

He had come home to Great Neck after losing the last job and they were making broad hints at him to move out again when he thought of it.

"Stanley, you're thirty years old in the spring," his mother had said. "You should be on your own." It had meant nothing to him. He couldn't conceive of the next year or the next. Doing what?

He knew they couldn't deny him this place for the winter. He would be out of their hair. How cold could it get? How lonely? He had always said he liked the winter beach best, to be perverse. Why not try it? He would throw parties. Stare at the Atlantic, gray-green like his eyes, he'd been told more than once. Catch up on his reading. Rest. His friends would come out from the city.

They didn't come out. In summer they stood in line, in winter they couldn't make it. They had season tickets to the opera, the Knicks, they had dinner parties, art openings, plays to see.

In November, when he moved in, the summer folks were gone. It was already winter. His mother had provided for him well, he decided after examining her newest purchases: pre-Columbian cats in odd corners, a freezer full of steak and fish sticks, six kinds of cookies, a full pantry, a full liquor cabinet, lobster from the Point.

*155*

She had redone the living room in white—white shag rug, white table and director's chairs, white wicker couch, glass and chrome coffee table, wicker liquor cabinet. Ridiculous in winter, all that wicker. Downstairs was still early American with colorful quilts in his old bedroom, his sister Jennie's room.

Later it became a challenge. The cold.

The storm in December was monstrous—the wind howling, the house shaking, waves pounding. He stayed wrapped in blankets, long underwear, jeans and several sweaters, his father's quilted parka, shivering all night in their bed, wondering if the water could reach him. Alone on the verge of that immense ocean, terrified. The year he was nine there had been a hurricane. The shoreline had shifted to within a stone's throw of the house.

At first, going into town for food was festive. He bought more lobster, cold cuts, smoked fish and bagels. They all asked about his father. "Sid coming out this weekend? Give him our love."

"Hey, kid, read in the *Times* his latest is gonna run forever. He's got the Midas touch on Broadway."

He went through all the meat in the freezer, halfway through the fish sticks before he got sick of them. Then canned consomme. Pasta with olive oil and garlic. He could taste corn on the cob with butter in his sleep.

He played all the records. Billy Joel, Elton John, the Beatles, a memorial of summers past. Then his mother's musical comedy albums, from *Oklahoma!* on. She had been on the stage briefly before she was married, she had performed in summer theater before the kids came. That's what gave his sister Margot the bug for acting. He listened to the tunes of all the years gone by. At last he narrowed it down to his favorite, *Man of La Mancha*, the side with "Impossible Dream," and sang along in his scratchy tenor. Margot had a glorious soprano. He had, they'd told him throughout his childhood, his mother's love of music, but not the talent. Just one more of those missing pieces that kept him from finding his place in the world.

He thought of his parents back in Great Neck. West Egg, it was. He used to go by Fitzgerald's house on the way to school. This was Fitzgerald country, a Fitzgerald fucking era.

He rummaged around in his old room. Hadn't his mother stored some of his college papers here? The significance of the green light in *Gatsby*. "So we beat on, boats against the current, borne back ceaselessly into the past." He was speaking aloud. He wanted to be borne back into the past. Into the 1920s, say, or back into the womb to start over.

He should have lived back then, he would have made out like a bandit. It was clear what a man should do, in those days. Today? Women. Work, the throb, the pursuit, for what? No one quite measured up to his private explorations. No one could please him the way he pleased himself. And the way women were today. Tougher than any of the men in the grey flannel suits, with their tortoise-shell glasses and their thighs lean from roadwork. They shook your hand, these days.

Where was the woman he could love, with her soft body and round face, her introverted streak. He would even prefer a Daisy, dressed and doted on by all those men. Or her friend the golfer, better than these tough women who all blurred together in his mind.

His mother had wanted him to do his master's thesis on James Joyce. She loved that Molly Bloom trash. He had stuck by F. Scott. "But he's such a light-weight," she protested.

His father said he was too romantic for his own good. "Toughen up," he said. "It's dog-eat-dog out there."

Now cousin Ben, there was an academic for you. The doors opened for him like magic. He fit the times. They needed a specialist in macroeconomic theory. Presto. Associate professor at twenty-six. And to think he used to imagine himself in the classroom teaching Bellow, Lessing and Chekhov, all those faces turned up to him. Even Mr. Chips had dignity. But he couldn't get even one part-time course to teach when he tried. Every prep school turned him down. In his extended cross-country job search he had learned that business courses were "impacted" with students, literature courses were "undersubscribed." No one cared about the liberal arts anymore.


The maid stopped coming in January or February. Too cold, or the beach road was too rough. Anyway, she stopped coming.

He wasn't messy, really, although the pizza boxes were hard to dispose of. Sometimes he made a bonfire on the beach.

The geography of the dunes changed each day. He searched in vain for the high dune he had jumped from as a child, giddy, panicked, forced onward by their jeers. Ben could do it. Even Margot, who was three years younger, could. He had to. It was a mountain of a dune. Then stinging pain, his ribs thrown against unyielding hardness, his teeth full of sand. Dizzy and betrayed, jumping up and running straight into the cold surf to hide his wet pants, his unmanly tears from the others.

He savored the memory of November, having a whole lobster to himself, digging out the steamer, the ritual of the kill, the flesh dripping in butter. He could imagine the taste of cold beer, hot sand, peaches.

He didn't walk the beach anymore. It was stinging cold out. The ocean roared. He dredged up more summer images, watching the Atlantic stormy gray. He found his old collections of seashells in a drawer. Jagged shells, razor sharp. He cut his feet.

After one terrible storm he was ill. The flu. Two weeks in their bed. Delirious. In the corner, Myron, Myron Gaiwo . . . Gaipong, Dipthing, Gawain, something like that, an insane chanting in his head, the words wouldn't come out right. Myron whatever-his-name-was contorted in the corner of their bedroom sucking his own cock. At boarding school they'd get drunk and go in a gang to Myron's room and he'd do it for a twenty.

In the corner of his parent's bedroom, decayed seagull carcasses, gnats and maggots on lustreless eyes, globs of sea jelly, tangles of seaweed. The sound of the pounding waves bored into his skull. Repetition maintained into infinity. He was so weary.

He examined the photo albums. His father with hair. His mother before puffy middle age. In some photos they were not much older than he. A typical family—a boy and a girl, a mother and father who worked hard and pushed them from Brooklyn to the suburbs in less than a generation. The beach house was the crowning glory.

The volleyball games, organized by summer folks, drinking and easy evenings. The kids in one crowd, playing at sunset in the surf, the gentle roar of grownup laughter in the background. The Atlantic stormy now, he loved it in its various moods.

The old men in shorts with gray, matted chests sipping gin on the porch watching the teenage girls with binoculars, cracking dirty jokes. He would hide under the porch and listen, trying to understand.

Photos of himself a scrawny ten. Stunted. Ben younger than he, eight then, already taller. Margie, who hadn't changed her name to Margot yet, was already a looker. She had her mother's pretty red hair and fair skin. His was curly and brown. He got the freckles.

Margie did what they told her. Puppet on a string, he called her. Now he slept in Margie's bed. After the storm he had left their bedroom alone. Crusted sheets, illness.

———————

Twelve weeks to go until warm weather. Or was it fifteen? He thought of buying a pair of sunglasses.

"Still here, then?" Tony, the grocer had said in January. And always after that, a perplexed look on his face. "Still here, then?" He wondered what he looked like.

He took to wearing a blanket for warmth, over his jeans and flannel bathrobe. He could nest in the blanket wherever he was, whenever he got tired. Always comfortable, yet presentable if someone came by.

No one came.

He had an assigned post, a director's chair in front of the picture window in the middle of the white living room with a broad view of the ocean beyond. He rarely left his post. He wrote STANLEY on the back of the chair in black magic marker.

He had discovered his own rhythm. Up at one or two, early afternoon, the brightest part of the day; to bed at five or six a.m. The bad hour, with its lukewarm irritating light. Some nights, when the roaring outside subsided, he found marvelous moments of peace. With the lights out he could catch the glimmer of the surf, a silver strip at the tideline. Listening to *La Mancha*. The moon was out often. The wind, always. Rattling and shivering. The city seemed far away. Five below. Minus thirty with wind chill factor. All that white wicker was blinding. He yearned for color.

At first the liquor cabinet held endless surprises. Liqueurs that tasted of the summer fruits—apricots, cherries, peaches, kiwi. Good, smooth scotch (his father's) that brought hours of tranquil gazing. A bottle of champagne left over from Margot and Jeremy's wedding reception. His little sister had eloped to City Hall with a Chicago actor who had a Tony and a recurring role as a second-string buddy in one of the sitcoms. When they found out, his folks were upset, but they threw them a party anyway. When he opened the bottle, the champagne was flat. But he drank it, iced in a silver bucket he found in one of the top shelves in the kitchen cupboard.

The champagne left him with a splitting headache. It was yeasty, bitter, as he sat listening to his dreams, the ocean, the grayness flooding him, and sandy shores treading through the center of his vision.

His mother: "Margot called. Jeremy has been invited to London to perform in a Pinter play. She's going along to study at the Royal Academy."

His father: "Margot hasn't done badly for herself. Now if my son would get settled I could rest easy."

His mother: "You're the dreamer, Margot is the doer."

His father: "Margot doesn't come home often enough to suit us. Of course, it's good she and Jeremy are so busy."

Tidepools in the corner, water spiders, crawdaddies.

He cut up Margot's sheets with the nail scissors he found in their bathroom. It took hours, off and on. He made tiny nicks in his hands, but that didn't stop him. He wiped them on Margot's colorful quilt, leaving it flecked with brown, creating a tweedy effect. A worthy occupation, he said to himself as he snipped away, softly at first, then loud, finally shouting, finding it hilarious. At last a worthy occupation.

One night he treated himself to a sixpack of Heineken. A sweet night, filled with memories of Roxanne. Near dawn, he called his friends in the city and announced he was getting married. Masterful. He turned their stunned sleepy anger into good wishes.

"Well, what do you know? Who's the lucky girl?" asked Ron, one of his graduate school classmates.

"Roxanne. I met her in London. She's flying here in June. We'll have a party out here, it will be beautiful then. You'll have to come meet her."

"You've been keeping yourself a secret," chided Sarah, from his second to last job. "Wait till I tell Sandy." Sandy was the boss who had forced him to leave. "This isn't working out," she had said. "I'm putting a warning in your personnel file." That meant he was supposed to leave before she fired him. To go where? Do what?

"Your parents must be kicking up their heels," said Jan. She had confided in him all last summer, when his father had gotten him a temporary job in the gift shop at the Museum of Modern Art.

"Have you found another job?" Jan probed.

"Who, me? Roxanne has money, didn't I tell you? I don't have to worry about that."

Finally he called Alan, his college roommate, in San Francisco. "What the fuck," Alan said as he picked up the phone.

"It's me, Stanley, what's happening?" He had to say it three times.

"Do you know it's three a.m.?" Alan sputtered. "Jesus, Stanley, you woke up the whole family." Alan and his wife Minky had two sons already in grade school. Alan had all the bases covered.

He hung up without telling him about the wedding.

How much longer? They must have all been wondering about him. "I've retired," he would tell them. "I'm withdrawing from the world. I've done it all, and it doesn't quite measure up."

It was true. He'd tried everything after drawing a blank with teaching jobs. Law school (he couldn't keep on top of the details of the LSATs), working in advertising (he wasn't quick enough to meet deadlines). F in life. Flunking out in the age of ambition.

The phone rang. Persistent, whoever it was. He counted to twenty-three.


He left his post only for food, drink, to use the bathroom, to shave. He considered devising a chamber pot to cut down on trips.

He arranged his dirty dishes on the carpet in orderly piles, subduing its brightness.

The dream? Leeches, sea slugs, in the hollow of his neck.

Roxanne liked the lights out. Mary liked him to use his tongue.

The wind whistled all night long. The waves crashed relentlessly. He bared his teeth from time to time.

His gray flannel robe and jeans. Barefoot. The blanket. His eyes were the same gray-green.

Something vicious.

"To dream the impossible dream." He sang along. Follow the bouncing ball.

He cut his feet on shells. The house creaked. He made lists. Tidal waves. How often? The probabilities? The contributing factors? An earthquake at sea, the encyclopedia said.

He went to bed after daybreak. He kept watch through the dark house, nocturnal as his mother's cats, sometimes in an eerie half sleep, half pleasant, floating. Sometimes he couldn't control the flow of his thoughts toward frothy sea broth, burrowing sand crabs, sea anemones pulsing and throbbing, a baby eel slithering along on its snout, jellyfish stinging his feet. The sound of water.

His eyes open, he saw his hand. That's the end of me. My extremity. In my extremity I see the end of me. Fingers, tentacles. The Atlantic is gray-green, the color of my eyes. Is anybody there?

He imagined a thirtieth birthday party. They would all cheer him, the people from everywhere in his path, filling the shorelines, a flood of people, clambering onto the porch for a closer look, half sinking in the sand, loaded down with platters of food, cold beer, gin and tonic.

Why go beyond? Nothing was ever as tasty as its anticipation.

He peopled the house with wits and voluptuaries. He found he need go no further than his own front door.

Women, the throb, the pursuit, for what?

He had lived with a girl once, a lovely girl. But she got on his nerves. At night he lay next to her, fighting the urge to slug her.

Sperm. The smell, the taste. How long did it take to dry?

"I've always loved the beach most in winter." He said it as an opening gambit at parties, throwing out bait. No one measured up.

He sat at his post, the gray-green Atlantic spread out before him. The waves arched higher and higher. The sound was gone now. He had erased it, the sound of the sea was gone. Soundlessly, he exulted. At last he had achieved a vacuum, a black hole of the mind.

The green light would come soon.

Jane Ciabattari was raised in Emporia, Kansas and studied creative writing at Stanford University and San Francisco State University. Her short stories have appeared in *Blueline*, *Caprice*, *Denver Quarterly*, *The East Hampton Star*, *Hampton Shorts* (which honored her with an Editors' Choice Stubby Award), *The North American Review* and *Redbook*, which nominated her for a National Magazine Award. She has been awarded fiction fellowships from The MacDowell Colony, the New York Foundation for the Arts and The Virginia Center for the Creative Arts. She is a Contributing Editor to *Parade* Magazine. With her husband Mark, who is also a writer, she divides her time between Sag Harbor, New York City and Windham, New York.

**List of our Literary Paperback Originals**

Anthony Brandt

*The People Along the Sand*. Three stories, six poems, a memoir. Tales of missed connections and misunderstandings, a memoir of the death of a marriage told with uncompromising honesty and uncommon grace. Introduction by Bill Henderson. $9.95. ISBN 0-9630164-1-5

Edward Butscher

*Child in the House*. A new collection of ferocious, yet human lyrics. Introduction by David Ignatow. $10.00 ISBN 0-9630164-9-0

Fran Castan

*The Widow's Quilt*. The center section of this moving collection of poems reflects the poet's experience as a woman made widow by the Vietnam War. Introduction by William Matthews. $12.00 ISBN 1-886435-04-9

Virginia Christian, Hope Harris, Erika Duncan

*Three Cautionary Tales*. Two novellas and one long short story explore that area where beauty and pain meet. $14.00 ISBN 0-9630164-3-1

Cyril Christo

*The Twilight Language.* First volume of poetry by a poet who, in the words of poet Hayden Carruth, "writes with the fire of youthful imagination and does it well." $12. ISBN 1-886435-05-7

Mark Ciabattari

*The Literal Truth: Rizzoli Dreams of Eating the Apple of Earthly Delights*. Surreal tales of Manhattan and the Hamptons. This "clever and cartoonish novel is a delightful romp, more Calvino than Kafka." –Kirkus Reviews $12 00 ISBN 0-9630164-7-4

### Pat Falk

*In The Shape of a Woman*. Poems by award-winner, Pat Falk. Introduction by Sidney Feshbach. "this is the form/we know where we are/we have come to speak through stone." $12.00 ISBN 1-886435-02-2

### Helen Ruth Freeman

*Diurnal Matters.* Foreword by Jean Valentine, who writes: "Here are poems that tell the story of a life–a woman's story..." written by "a wry, observant poet, intelligent, shrewd with self-irony..." $13.00 ISBN 1-886435-08-1

### Dan Giancola

*Powder and Echo: Poems about the American Revolutionary War on Long Island.* Stirring monologues by historic figures rendered in poetry. Introduction by Edward Butscher. $9.95 ISBN 0-9630164-0-7

### Jennie Hair

*A Sisterhood of Songs*. Poems about women. "Is there something/that makes it necessary for us to be protected–/something implicit/in the hand under the elbow/as we cross the street/" Introduction by Maxwell Corydon Wheat, Jr. $11.00 ISBN 1-886435-00-6

### William Hathaway

*Sightseer.* Poems simultaneously comic and tragic, satiric and idealistic, intellectual and vulgar, formal and colloquial. $14.00 ISBN 1-886435-10-3

### Peter Lipman-Wulf

*Period of Internment: Letters and Drawings from Les Milles 1939-1940*. A memoir of a German-born American sculptor who was interned at Camp Les Milles in southern France with other German Jews, artists and intellectuals at the outbreak of World War II. $15.00 ISBN 0-9630164-5-8

### Robert Long

*Blue*. Poems of New York City and Eastern Long Island "Cross the hilarity of Cummings with the intelligence of Proust and ardor of Cavafy, and you've begun to outline his powers."–Mary Karr.$14.00 ISBN 1-886435-09-X

### Daniel Thomas Moran

***In Praise of August***. Poems about growing up on Long Island in an Irish-American milieu by the popular, lively host of *The Long Island Radio Magazine* who practices Dentistry on Shelter Island when not writing poems. $15.00 ISBN 1-886435-07-3

### Allen Planz

***Dune Heath***. The poet's passion for the sea and nature reflect his passion for life and love. In the words of Peter Matthiessen, these poems "invigorate the grit and feel of the South Fork waters...and bring to life the shapes and silhouettes of the wild things flying beneath the sparkling surface as well as over it." $15. ISBN 1-886435-06-5

### Davida Singer

***Shelter Island Poems***. Poems about love and a spiritual journey. "I want to be past you/as the angle of white sail/slips across the bay/just until sunset/without words and is gone" Forward by Erika Duncan. $11.00 ISBN 1-886435-01-4

### Rob Stuart

***Similar to Fire.*** In the Forward the poet writes: "Language is the refining fire of my soul, and poetry is its most intimate voice...Poetry is passing the fire hand to hand, soul to soul." Introduction by Perdita Schaffner. $10.95 ISBN 0-9630164-2-3

### Pat Sweeney

***A Thousand Times and Other Poems***. A stunning collection which celebrates "love, sex, a body that is alive, the quickened pulse, the inevitability of longing and desire," as described in the Introduction by R.S.Jones. $10.00 ISBN 0-9630164-8-2

### Sandra Vreeland

***The Sky Lotto***. Poems with an introduction by Barbara Guest who says, "I am shy before these poems written so close to the heart." Vreeland received the Extraordinary Voice Award from Mother's Voices for giving children the opportunity to express their thoughts about AIDS in verse which was then published by The Poetry Society of America $12.00 ISBN 1-886435-03-0

Beverley Wiggins Wells

***Simply Black***. With a focus upon race and gender, these are poems in which the poet is in touch with a "consciousness empowering me/to be ultimately whole/hyphen free/like the color of the cosmos/simply black." Introduction by Suzanne Gardinier. $10.00 ISBN 0-9630164-4-X

### *For David Ignatow: An Anthology*

Forty-seven poets celebrate the birthday of one of America's most distinguished poets. Among the contributors are: Philip Appleman, Marvin Bell, Siv Cedering, Diana Chang, Paul Mariani, Joyce Carol Oates, Diane Wakoski. $10.00 ISBN 0-9630164-6-6